Annabelle du Fouet

Weather Balloons Make ROTTEN Sex Toys

Cerridwen Press

A Cerridwen Press Publication

www.cerridwenpress.com

Weather Balloons Make Rotten Sex Toys

ISBN #1419954830

Edited by Mary Moran
Cover art by Syneca

Electronic book Publication May 2005
Trade Paperback Publication July 2006

Cerridwen Press is an imprint of Ellora's Cave Publishing, Inc.®

About the Author

Annabelle du Fouet lives in a small mid western town with her three cats, Aristotle, Socrates and PeeWee. She used to have a parrot named Stalin but he died. Until recently, she was actively involved in her local gardening club, a film appreciation society and a book club. Annabelle holds a PhD in General Studies from Indiana University. Weather Balloons Make Rotten Sex Toys is her first book, although she has created the index for several academic works, including *Sailing Among the Savages: Cannibalism in Upper Michigan* and *Pornographic Icons: Why Donald Duck Never Wears Pants.*

Actually, Annabelle inhabits the mind of a real woman who has two children but no cats or parrots, dead or otherwise. She did earn a boring PhD that has nothing to do with sex, kink or romance. This real woman has never worn a latex catsuit or flogged anyone, but she has visited a dungeon and seen many strange things from her vantage point in a safe corner.

Annabelle welcomes comments from readers. You can find her website and email address on her author bio page at www.cerridwenpress.com

Weather Balloons Make Rotten Sex Toys

Introduction

How this book came to be

INSPIRATION FROM UNCLE HENRY

It was a year ago that Uncle Henry disappeared. He just didn't come home one day and no one has heard from him since. My heart goes out to dear Aunt Ruth, who immediately went into hysterics. She cried not one tear over losing her beloved spouse of some thirty-five years. Instead, she spent her days smiling and laughing as though she were the happiest woman in the world. We begged her to get counseling but she only grinned and went on about how wonderful life had become. Poor woman.

Not long after Uncle Henry vanished, Aunt Ruth called and asked me to come over and sort through his belongings. "I want his shit out of here," she told me, "but I don't want to touch any of that slimy rat bastard's crap myself. I need you to take care of it."

Of course, it was the hysteria making her talk about her soul mate that way. Although I did not relish the idea of going through Uncle Henry's personal things, my heart went out to dear Aunt Ruth and I knew I had to help. Besides, I needed something to occupy me. My efforts to find employment as a professional researcher had been, to say the least, mysteriously unsuccessful, despite the fact that I hold a Ph.D. in Sociology from Indiana University and had once helped my faculty advisor create the index for one of her many scholarly books.

Armed with many empty boxes, I went to my aunt's home where she met me at the door with a radiant smile. The doctor must have given her tranquilizers to ease her pain, I thought, making a mental note to go along with whatever Aunt Ruth wanted, lest the hysterics recur.

"What do you think?" Aunt Ruth asked, pointing to her head. She'd changed her hair color from a mousey brown to a brilliant red, styled in a dramatic upsweep. She'd also started wearing makeup, with heavy blue eye shadow, thick false eyelashes and bright red lipstick, all of which clashed with the tight purple flowered dress she'd wedged her chubby body into.

"Um, it's very nice," I lied, trying not to upset her delicate mental state.

Pointing a pudgy finger at Uncle Henry's den, Aunt Ruth gave me orders. "Pack it all up and burn it. Just set fire to it and stomp on the ashes. Put a wooden stake through it all. Pour acid on it. I don't care."

Lugging a suitcase from her bedroom, Aunt Ruth told me she was leaving the house in my care while she vacationed in the Bahamas. She stopped to primp in front of the hallway mirror then kissed her reflection, leaving a red lip print.

A car horn tooted in the driveway. "Antonio is right on time," Aunt Ruth beamed. Grabbing the suitcase, she hauled it to the door where Antonio waited. He was a short, thin man with greasy black hair and a pencil moustache, wearing tight pants and a shirt unbuttoned almost to the navel. Aunt Ruth said he was some sort of massage therapist who'd been treating her bad back. The young man embraced her warmly and whispered something in her ear, making Aunt Ruth giggle.

As Antonio hauled the suitcase to the car, Aunt Ruth gave me another gleaming smile. "I'll be gone for quite a long time, Annabelle. Do take care of the house for me like a good girl and don't forget to clear Henry's wretched things out of here." After giving me a loving peck on the cheek, poor distraught Aunt Ruth strode away, humming a tune to herself.

As the roar of Antonio's sports car faded in the distance, I looked sadly around the house once so full of love and gaiety, and now filled with the gloom of a wonderful marriage brought down in its prime. With a heavy heart, I began the task of removing Uncle Henry's belongings from his former home.

Bookshelves lined Uncle Henry's den, not surprising since he read voraciously. Glancing at the hundreds of books, I decided to pack them first and as I pulled the volumes from the shelves one-by-one, I couldn't help but glance at some of the titles. *The ABCs of BDSM.* Uncle Henry always did like word games. *Fun with Whips.* Obviously, some sort of cookbook about dessert toppings. *Leather and Loving It.* I remembered Aunt Ruth going on about how Uncle Henry was a "leather freak" and how he liked to hang out with his "sick chums". Knowing Uncle Henry, he probably liked to make craft items for friends who were in the hospital.

As I continued packing, I noticed a theme. Many of the books featured scantily clad women on the dust jackets and some had covers showing what appeared to be men dressed as women, always with a stern lady standing nearby, holding a whip. As I am not as naive as some people think, I'm aware some men like to dress in female clothing but the presence of the whip-wielding women puzzled me. Perhaps the men in the pictures had stolen the clothing from the women, who used the whips to ensure the return of their belongings. Using a whip seemed a drastic measure but as any woman knows, clothes are very expensive.

As explicit as the books were, they were tame compared to the magazines stored in the back of Uncle Henry's closet. All of them had extremely graphic covers, usually featuring menacing leather-clad women engaged in mean-spirited activities at the expense of apparently helpless men. They (the magazines, not the men) had exotic titles: *Leather Bitches from Hell, Goddess Betty and Her Amazon Army, Made Into a Maid,* on and on it went, all with the same general theme.

Later still, I discovered a cache of DVD's hidden behind a row of encyclopedias. They were just as explicit as the magazines, judging from the covers. *Genitals Prefer Blondes, Attack of the Bloodthirsty She-Devils, Whipped Into Shape,* and *Mister Chipmunk Gets Some Wood,* were just a few I saw, although that last title may well have been a children's video.

It took quite a few boxes to get all of Uncle Henry's materials packed away. When I finished, my spirits felt as empty as the den but I didn't have time to brood because I had to figure out what to do with everything I'd amassed. It seemed a shame to throw away Uncle Henry's things, weird as they might be, so I hired a man to truck them to my home, where I had them placed in my ample basement storage room.

Weeks went by. I heard little from Aunt Ruth, save for the occasional postcard from the Bahamas. Obviously, her emotional wounds still festered because many of her postcards made little sense, like this one:

Dearest Annabelle,

Having a splendid time! Last night I did a sixty-nine with Antonio that went on for HOURS. Later I even let him go in my back door, if you know what I mean, wink wink. I love that man's tool so much!

Much Love,

Aunt Ruth

I didn't know much about Antonio but with the talk of back doors and tools, I figured he must be a handyman of some sort. Perhaps they had rented a cottage that needed repairs. Anyway, I knew that even though Aunt Ruth needed desperately to talk about Uncle Henry, it must have been too painful to do so, since she never mentioned him in any of her postcards. Such a sad thing.

After the excitement involving my aunt and uncle, life settled into a routine once again but I found myself often drifting into a reverie, thinking about the odd materials packed away in my basement. Something about the books, magazines and videos intrigued me, despite my initial discomfort with their content. Obviously, Uncle Henry wasn't alone in his strange interests. Since he was able to amass such a large collection of materials, there must be others very much like him.

My intellectual curiosity finally got the best of me one evening, so I went to the basement and opened a box at random. Sitting in an old recliner that had long ago been relegated downstairs, I started to read some of Uncle Henry's books and magazines. Perhaps knowing something of his interests would enable me to know him better. Maybe I could even figure out what caused his sudden disappearance.

Before long, my scholarly instincts rose to the surface and I found myself eagerly consuming the contents of box after box, exulting in the process of learning. However, I must admit what I read appalled me, at least at first. Why would women want to treat men so horribly, beat them with whips, tie them up, force them to wear women's clothing? Adding to my confusion was the arcane lingo used in the books and magazines. With my extensive background in linguistics, however, I was soon able to grasp the meaning of such terms as *bitch goddess, golden showers* (ick!), *rim job* (ick! ick!) and *scat* (triple ick!).

I spent many evenings in that recliner, pouring over the vast array of materials at hand. As time went on, I realized I'd become obsessed with "the world of kink," as I came to think of it. I gave up all other activities in order to further my research, too busy either reading about kink or watching it on one of Uncle Henry's many videos.

I began to receive phone calls from my friends at the canasta club, wondering if I was okay. The chairwoman of the Harold Leipnitz Film Appreciation Society came to visit, wanting to know why I'd missed so many meetings, especially the one where it was my turn to bring coffeecake. That particular visit did not go well, as I had absent-mindedly answered the door holding a copy of *Lactating Dommes* magazine, the cover featuring a large-breasted woman squirting milk on a bound and gagged male slave. From chairwoman's chilly reaction, I knew it would be some time before the Leipnitz Society welcomed me back.

After weeks of serious study, I was surprised to find one evening that I had exhausted every box of Uncle Henry's kinky collection. Strangely enough, I felt a letdown, knowing I had nothing left to study.

Or did I?

An idea formed and took hold. After studying Uncle Henry's material, I figured I'd become something of an expert in the ways of kink. Certainly, I would never do such things myself but as a trained researcher, I possessed the ability to analyze my data and present it to a new audience that, like me, had never heard of the kinky subculture. The idea grew on me, almost like a garden fungus, and thus was born the idea for this book.

Even though my primary purpose was to make a serious scientific study of the kinky world, I have to admit that thoughts of Uncle Henry were in the back of my mind. I thought it might help alleviate the pain of losing him by sharing his world with others.

The initial results of my extensive content analysis of Uncle Henry's materials were quite good, but it seemed as though something was lacking. I puzzled over this for some time until I realized that despite my considerable analytical skills, the results were somewhat sterile, for lack of a better term. My research material was of a highly personal nature and my findings needed to reflect that. Therefore, I decided to engage in an ethnographic study. For those of you who don't have a Ph.D., I should explain that ethnography is concerned with describing the traits of groups of people. This technique, I felt, would supply the missing bit of intimate understanding that could only be obtained by immersing myself in the dark kinky realm that so fascinated dear Uncle Henry.

Since proper ethnography requires participation in the group under study, I insinuated myself into the kink community. This necessity both intrigued and horrified me—particularly the latter, since I had no desire to be chased by a fiend wielding a riding crop or speargun.

I faced an additional problem in that I had almost no firsthand experience with abnormal behavior so I wasn't entirely sure what role I should take as a community member. Finally, I took my inspiration from one of Uncle Henry's magazines, *Bum Bashing Vixens from Hell Itself,* and decided to assume a role as a dominatrix. I chose the moniker Mistress Yolanda, Empress of Uneasiness, which for some reason inspired much giggling amongst my fellow dominatrixes. I then christened myself Lady Umbrage but no one seemed to understand what that meant. For a brief time I became Madame Shirley, the Vexatious Domme, but many people somehow got the idea I had some sort of viral illness and wouldn't allow me to come near them.

Finally, I found a successful title: Mistress Dominique, Queen of Discomfort, and in such guise I was able to penetrate the closely guarded kinky community. (The impulse to write "kinky kommunity" is almost overwhelming but that wouldn't be very professional of me, would it?) I wish I could say my foray into perversion was entirely enjoyable but it wouldn't be the truth. Much of what goes on in the shadowy realm in which I found myself is difficult to understand. The rules of behavior are strict and yet at the same time there was little effort to educate *newbies* such as myself as to the expected codes of conduct. More often than I care to remember, the phrase "what the hell are you doing?" was hurled my way, along with such epithets as "dumbass" and "stupid bitch". Certainly, my feelings were hurt but when doing an ethnographic study of this scope, you have to accept the good with the bad and keep pushing forward.

It took nearly a year to gather the information I needed to publish this research. I traveled the country, visiting all manner of kinky venues: dungeons, bed and bondage inns, seedy bars, large conventions, and everything in between. Despite the popular conception of kinky people as mouth-breathing sex fiends, I found my new companions to be as diverse as any other subculture one might find in this country. Pervs—as they like to call themselves—come from all walks of life, all social strata and every ethnic background you could imagine. As a result, my work turned out to be as much a portrait of the Great American Melting Pot as anything else, although this particular pot happened to include people rather fond of whips, handcuffs and latex, among other things.

Now my research is done and I present not only my findings but a comprehensive guide to all things kinky. By now, you've likely noticed that the word *kinky* keeps popping up in this introduction, as it does throughout the book.

You're probably wondering, "What the heck is kinky stuff, anyway?" Well, it's lots of things. For some people, it's anything your parents wouldn't do. Let's face it; the thought of your leather-clad mother chasing your father—wearing a mask and a feather boa—around the bedroom with a riding crop is really disgusting.

Oh dear, now I'm thinking about it. I need to sit down and put a cold cloth on my head.

Okay. All better.

For other people, kinky means the standard "whips and chains" cliché you hear so often. It's not clear how those two items came to represent kink. Why not ball gags and nipple clamps? Floggers and cuffs? Tire irons and pillows? Well, maybe not that last one. Anyway, this definition of kink implies that sex toys of some kind are involved, which is indeed the case, as we'll discover.

There are those who think that being kinky means to be bereft of morals and believe that kinky folk are likely to engage in mass orgies and indiscriminate sex with total strangers or perhaps even household pets. That's probably more a definition of what goes on every Friday night in a frat house. Happily, it applies to a much lesser extent in the kinky community.

In a broad sense, some people think that kink is anything other than sex between married, heterosexual people using only the missionary position. Forget that. For one thing, I've been unable to discover just who these missionaries were and why a sex position was named for them. Apparently, they must have liked to "get it on," as the kids say, but other than that, we know almost nothing. Repeated calls and faxes to Jerry Falwell's office for clarification on this missionary thing failed to produce any sort of a response, aside from a threatening letter from his attorney.

It's starting to look like *kink* is a slippery concept. Let's assume it has nothing whatsoever to do with your parents. Let's get that image out of our heads right now. It doesn't matter that once you snooped through your parents' drawers and found a bullwhip, a steel collar and a pair of size thirteen-wide pink patent leather pumps. We don't want to think about such things. It's not good to think about such things. Not good at all.

Come to think of it, it's not that important to come up with a definitive meaning for kinkiness. Kink is in the eye of the beholder. It's a shadowy subculture of people doing all kinds of interesting things with other people, using an endless array of exotic devices, up to and including Nixon masks and stuffed kitties. There's leather clothing, latex clothing, satin clothing, spandex clothing, no clothing. There are bankers, doctors, teachers, truck drivers, housewives, insurance agents, international spies, you name it. There are people named Mistress Darkside, Master Claw and Señor Dave.

Kink is like Soylent Green. It's made of people! PEEEOPLE! (Since this is a book you'll have to imagine my eerily accurate Charlton Heston impersonation. I will say without modesty that my friends enjoy it very much.)

More than anything else, in reading this book you will encounter an amazing array of people and the activities that comprise kinky behavior. Perhaps you will learn about things you never dreamed possible. You may find yourself titillated or even disgusted. Regardless, as far as I can tell, this work is the most exhaustive and accurate research project ever undertaken on the subject. In the end, my wish is that you find this research interesting, informative and hopefully of some use in your daily lives. Just don't let your children read this, at least until they're eighteen. Really. I'm not kidding.

Chapter One

Kinksters and kinksterettes—Who are these people, anyway?

KINK 101

If we want to understand kinky behavior, we must develop an understanding of the people behind the behavior. After all, it's all about people, right? Okay, it's also about floggers, rubber clothes, weird shoes, industrial-sized cans of baked beans and metal things with spikes sticking out of them. But it's mostly about people.

First, we need to define what *kink* is, since we really didn't get around to that in the introduction. I must admit I wasn't quite sure what the word meant when I started this odyssey, so I looked it up in my Oxford English Dictionary. I was a bit put off at what I found: *An asymmetric, linear zone of deformation characterized by short fold limbs and very small hinge zones. Kink bands commonly occur as conjugate sets (see Conjugate Fold).* Well, this sounded not only awful but a bit obtuse as well. What on earth is a conjugate fold?

Fortunately, I soon realized I had found the entry for something called a "kink band," which probably refers to that awful Marilyn Manson woman the kids around here blast on their hi-fis all day long.

Let's try again. A more careful inspection of the dictionary reveals that kink is defined as *a sexual deviant or someone who has a sexual perversion or perverse idiosyncrasy.* That sounds a bit sinister, does it not? It's also troubling, as Aunt Ruth often referred to her husband as a "fat kinky bastard". That doesn't fit my memory of dear Uncle Henry, who didn't seem sinister at all. But who am I to fuss with the dictionary? Or Aunt Ruth, for that matter.

Armed with a definition, we can now begin our investigation into kinkiness. Naturally, the first thing we want to know is how to identify kink when we see it. This is problematic. At first, I assumed there was only one way to be kinky. This turned out to be a wildly erroneous assumption. There are, in fact, 52,238 different ways to express your particular kink. (I know this because I counted them, with the help of Stacey Smith-Bajorek, a divorcée from down the street.)

With so many deviant behaviors to choose from, you may wonder if anyone shares your particular kink. Hah! Rest assured, if you can think up a barmy turn-on, so can someone else. They're out there, somewhere, waiting to meet you. Do you have a fetish for end tables? Check the Internet. I'll bet there are at least a hundred sites created for people just like you. But what if you're sexually aroused by the idea of making love in a giant vat of cottage cheese? A little searching will reveal you're not alone, even though that kink sounds pretty stupid when you get right down to it.

Keep your eyes open! Maybe that nice man at the bank explaining why your account is overdrawn again is wearing rubber diapers under his pinstriped suit. Or perhaps your beautician is sexually excited by lava lamps. And who knows what lurks in the minds of politicians? That's an area even I don't want to explore. (For more information on finding fellow kinksters, see Chapter Seven, Finding Kink.)

Most kinky activities fall under the behavioral umbrella of **BDSM**—pronounced BUD-ism, a tribute to one of the early practitioners of kinky behavior, Donatien Alphonse Francois "Bud" de Sade. Don't confuse BDSM with Buddhism, which doesn't involve a lot of leather equipment, chains or people named Lord SteelThunder. BDSM takes its name from the people credited with starting various kinky activities. The "**B**" means **bondage**, which, as we all know, is the derivation of sexual pleasure from either tying people up or having them tie you up.

The concept of sexual bondage originates with a man known as Tim the Depraved, who lived in Blemsplut, a village in some foreign country back in the second century. (At one point I'd written down which foreign country but now I can't find that piece of paper. It was some Godforsaken place nobody cares about so let's not worry about it.) From ancient scrolls found only a few years ago, scholars discovered a tale concerning Tim's exploits, in which he herded a thousand cattle for many miles without one beast dying on the way.

This, obviously, has nothing to do with bondage, so now it seems completely unclear why Tim would be associated with it. It sounded good when the story was posted on the Internet, but it was late and your author had spent too many hours in front of the computer that day. Oh well. Onward and upward.

Next, we have the "**D**" in BDSM, which stands for discipline. Fortunately, this has nothing to do with that confusing stuff about Tim the Depraved. My linguistics training tells me that *discipline* stems from the Latin word *diss*, which means "to put down," and from the Greek word *cipline*, which refers to a group of mothers who sat on rocks singing sweet songs to sailors passing by. Logically, it follows that *discipline* means, "to put down someone's mother".

The first use of discipline is associated with ancient Roman generals, who liked to yell obscenities at their troops. From what I can make out of the admittedly sparse records of this period, these obscenities involved some aspect of the troops' mothers' personal hygiene or sexual preferences.

What is not clear is why the Roman generals would do this or what positive benefit the practice had in training soldiers. Even so, to this day the act of discipline is reserved for those people whose particular kink involves dressing up like a Roman soldier and getting yelled at by someone dressed as a Roman general.

Moving on, we have "**S**," which stands for **sadist**, a term coined from one of the earliest practitioners of sadistic behavior, the Marquis de Sadist, a mean, creepy person who liked to hit people with whatever object lay at hand—bottles, rocks, small dogs, etc. Soon enough, his friends learned to keep a safe distance from the Marquis but that only caused him to start throwing objects at them. Luckily, he had extremely poor aim and rarely hit his target.

The Marquis' kinky career came to an abrupt end when he was thrown in prison, probably because people got sick and tired of ducking flying shoes and end tables all the time. (My friend Gisele says the Marquis quit because he developed a rotator cuff injury. I'm not sure if she's kidding or not.) Toward the end of his life, the Marquis joined forces with a man named Queensberry; together they invented the rules for boxing or the Marquis and Queensberry Rules, which have been followed by every boxer to this day except Mike Tyson, who broke the rule about not biting the other guy's ear off.

Finally, we have "**M**," or **masochism**, a word derived from another man who lived in the past, Baron Leopold von Masochism. He was the polar extreme of the Marquis de Sadist in that he didn't like hurting other people. Instead, he liked for other people to hurt him. If the Baron lived today, he would likely be a professional wrestler named Scrap Iron Morwitzski or some such thing. He'd throw all his bouts, letting such opponents as The Atomic Skull or Mr. Death whack him over the head with folding chairs and break most of his bones. And he'd be as happy as a clam. As it is, the

Baron died quite some time ago, after falling through a window after cutting himself shaving. One can only presume he died smiling.

Today, masochists are often employed as telemarketers or technical support people at Internet service providers. These unique occupations require people to spend their days being yelled at or hung up on by angry people they don't know.

You may wonder, if a person is interested in "B," does it mean they are necessarily interested in "D" as well? No. For example, a person might be attracted to "B" and "S" but not "D" and "M," which would make their kink "BS." My research shows that most of the people involved in this derivation are attorneys and politicians, for some odd reason. These people also tend to be into "B" and "M," or "BM," which sounds truly disgusting and won't be discussed here.

In addition to BDSM, the kink world is a veritable alphabet soup of activities. Listed below are only a few of the many commonly used acronyms:

BJ: I heard this term frequently on my research travels, usually contained in a sentence such as: "Hey baby, how about a BJ?" As far as I can tell, it must refer to a bologna and jelly sandwich.

BT: Ball torture. I was never able to discern if this pertains to a certain type of ball, such as a baseball or tennis ball, or is an all-inclusive term for any ball.

CBT: Cock-and-ball torture. Ball torture again but this time including a rooster in the act, I believe. Someone will have to explain how this works.

CP: Corporal punishment. Why corporals? Why not sergeants or captains? May be involved in the military aspect of **discipline**, as noted above.

GS: Golden showers. As far as I can tell, this has something to do with utilizing honey while taking a shower. Perhaps it's good for the hair.

PA: Prince Albert. I know England's royal family has had their problems, but I have a hard time envisioning this fine gentleman dressed in rubber and clutching a riding crop while chasing the Queen around Buckingham Palace.

T&A: "Gimme some T&A!" Men yelled that at me on more than one occasion during my travels researching this book. I believe it's tavern lingo for a drink popular with kinksters (tea and avocado juice?), but when I asked about this, the men just laughed.

WS: Water sports. Perhaps this explains the fuss kinksters make about rubber outfits. My understanding is that surfers often wear rubberized "wetsuits" to maintain their body temperature while in the water. It may be that kinksters put those wetsuits to their own nefarious purposes. Or, water sports may refer to a kinky activity that goes on while waterskiing. I never observed this kink though I very much wanted to.

THE PEOPLE BEHIND THE KINK

What makes kinky people tick? Is it the desire for cheap thrills? The idea of flaunting social morés? The restless desire for something different than traditional sexual practices? There are more questions than answers, as we will discover in the course of this book. Still, we must begin somewhere, so I decided to start with the simple question, "Why?"

It was my good fortune, at the outset of this research, to overhear a married kinky couple, Misty and George, talking at the grocery store. Mustering my courage, I approached them in my Mistress Dominique persona and explained my project. They agreed to talk with me right there in the fruit and produce section.

Mistress Dominique: So, why are you kinky?

Misty: It started when George stayed up late one night, watching some movie on HBO. There was a scene in the movie where a woman tied up a man and whacked him good with a cat-o'-nine-tails. The next morning he told me he had a woody that wouldn't stop.

Public address system: Cleanup in aisle five. Cleanup in aisle five, please.

MD: Did this excite you as well?

Misty: Heck, no. I told him he was crazy if he wanted me to hit him with something made from cats. I like cats!

George: I had to explain that a cat-o'-nine-tails isn't made from cats. I think it's woodchucks or something.

Misty: Who cares about woodchucks? When I realized no cats were involved, I told George we'd give it a try.

George: Our sex life was pretty boring at that time.

Misty: No kidding. The kinky stuff's brought back all the excitement, just like the first time we did it in the dumpster behind that McDonald's.

George: We're still working on some of the details, though.

MD: Oh?

George: Well, Misty—I call her Mistress ThunderThigh when we're doing it—she likes to whip me but she always makes me take aspirin first so it won't hurt so much. I keep telling her it's *supposed* to hurt but she doesn't listen.

Misty: Hey, I hurt you the other day, didn't I?

George: Yeah, but that was when you accidentally pinned me between the car and the garage door. That wasn't kinky.

Public address system: Attention, shoppers! For the next five minutes, chicken potpies are two for a dollar in the frozen food section. That's chicken potpies, folks—you don't want to miss out!

MD: Have you met any other kinky couples?

George: Not really. One night I was down at Lucky's Bar hoisting a couple of brewskis when I heard a guy talking about swinging a cat at his girlfriend. I got interested for a minute, but then it turned out he was talking about hitting his girlfriend with a real cat.

Misty: I told you! People watch those cable movies and then the next you know, some poor animal's getting used as a weapon.

George: Well, he's in jail now. Looks like it's against the law to hit anyone with a cat.

Misty: Good.

As we can see from this brief interview, the decision to enter the kinky lifestyle is not an easy one. My experience tells me, however, that if kinky people are anything, they are a determined lot. The ship of kink sails troubled waters indeed but sail on it does.

KINKY GROUPINGS

At its most simple, a kinky relationship consists of a dominant person and a submissive person, or a **top** and a **bottom**. We can think of them by which end of a whip they're on. The top is the one holding the handle of a whip, while the bottom gets the business end of the thing. Of course, a top is a person who shares a mindset with the aforementioned Marquis de Sadist, while a bottom shares the desires of that Baron Masochist person.

In the course of my research, I also spoke to a few people who claimed to be **switches** but this makes no sense. A switch is an implement used by a top to punish a bottom, which has nothing to do with the role played by a person in a kinky act. They might as well claim to be a baseball bat or a flamethrower.

It gets even more complicated. Many tops refer to themselves as a **dom** (if they're male) or **domme** (female) or even **domdomme** if they're one of those transformers who get confused about the gender thing. A neophyte kinkster should learn early on how to distinguish between a dom and a domme if one wishes to avoid trouble. One easy way to make the distinction is by asking the dominant their name. If the name begins with *Sir,* chances are you've got a dom. Similarly, if the name begins with *Lady,* the person is quite likely a domme. I don't know what to tell you about the transformers.

It should be noted that the title adopted by a dominant often indicates some aspect of their kinky role, meaning that the name must be selected with great care. The goal is to select a name that will inspire fear and respect in the bottoms. At least I *think* that's the idea. I'm probably missing something but I fail to see how calling oneself Master Poopchute would inspire such awe, however, one night in Florida I watched subs follow this Poopchute person all over a dungeon, desperately trying to get his attention. Go figure.

Through my research, I discovered the steps by which the dominant title is created:

First, the kinky person decides whether they are dominant or submissive. If they are dominant, they proceed to the next step. If they are submissive, they should not read the information below, which is intended only for dominant persons and professional researchers such as myself.

If the person is male, he determines whether he wishes to be called *Lord, Sir,* or *Master.* A dominant female chooses from *Lady, Mistress,* or *Ms.* It's very important to have some sort of title to indicate your role, otherwise a dominant might be taken as a submissive and find him- or herself fighting off the advances of other dominants armed with riding crops and ballpeen hammers.

No self-respecting dom or domme would want to be known as Sir Hubert or Mistress Hortense. Therefore, a fierce moniker must be selected. The most popular choices are those that imply power and/or evil. This is why so many doms are called Master Unpleasant, Sir Lash-a-Lot or Lord Supreme Ruler of the Universe. Likewise, many dommes opt for such names as Mistress Savage, Lady Surly or Ms. Spiteful. Sometimes a compound name is used, such as Lord IronWad or Lady CrazedPsycho.

Titles are not an important issue with submissives. Many times their dominant will choose a name for them, such as My Little Poopy Drawers or Vermin Boy. If a submissive is unattached, they may select a name that best expresses their particular kinky desires, such as Monkey Boffer or Mr. Pee. (I'm told that the latter name indicates someone who likes to drink urine. Urine? Good lord!)

In the course of my travels I noticed many subs had pet names for their dom/mes, the most popular being "asshole," "dumbass" and "shit-for-brains". There seems to be a theme here, possibly linked to potty training but that's an area I was not able to pursue to any great degree.

When kinky relationships were still a new thing—in approximately 612 BC, before kink was all over the Internet and some of the smuttier cable networks—people would often get confused and a dominant would end up with another dominant or a submissive with another submissive. Not only did this prove unsatisfying in terms of anyone getting their needs met, it turns out that while submissives often get along quite well with one another, dominants tend to despise other dominants. This transcript from one of the sessions of the Professional Order of Perverts (POOP) convention is illustrative:

"Good evening, and welcome to the Professional Order of Perverts' International Council of Masters. I am your leader, Lord ThunderSteel."

"Leader? The hell you are!"

"Yeah, who died and made you boss? How would you like a taste of the whip, big boy?"

"I am Sir SteelThunder! I take orders from no one, especially Lord ThunderSteel! On your knees, pretender to the throne!"

"Shut up, male worm! I am Mistress Steel Heel! No puny male will ever rule the Council of Masters!"

"A mere woman dares to speak without permission? Assume position 35.6 as described in the Gor manual! Or was that the Klingon dictionary? I forget."

"Ahoy, mateys. I be Captain Tidepool, master of the good ship Wynona. Where be the seminar on keelhauling? Arrrrr."

"Everyone shut up! Lord ThunderSteel commands it! I am your leader! I have this badge that says so!"

"We don't need no stinking badges!"

"My badge says I'm the Emperor."

"Shut up, you twerp."

"Everybody shut up! I got a tattoo on my butt that says I'm Lord ThunderEmperor!"

"I'll tattoo your butt, you slimy piece of male shit. Get on your knees and worship my heels!"

"Go make me some coffee, bitch!"

"That's it! I've had it! Stand still while I stick these needles in your inferior male scrotum!"

"Come on, everyone! Pleeeeaase! Just let me be the leader! Do you know how much time it took me to think up the name Lord ThunderSteel? That ought to count for something!"

The transcript goes on in this manner for many pages, until it suddenly stops when the local police break in and haul everyone off to jail for disturbing the peace. This is not an isolated incident by any means but seems to be fairly indicative of what occurs when dominants are left to themselves in closed quarters.

Polyamory: Many in today's society believe that the only proper relationship consists of a man and a woman in a monogamous, heterosexual coupling. As you might expect, this does not hold true in the world of kink. Just about any conceivable type of relationship can be found, so when you speak of a "couple," it may refer to a man and a woman, or two men, or two women or some other thing if one of those transformers is involved.

Making the situation more complicated is the fact that more than a few people in kinkdom prefer a **polyamorous** relationship, which might include one man and two or more women, or vice versa. Or maybe three men and one woman, or five men and four women. Or maybe—well, you get the idea. I haven't had time to check this out thoroughly but apparently the concept of polyamory was borrowed from the Amish, one of the very few contributions they've made to kinky culture. The Amish are also the inspiration for the frequent inclusion of butter churns in kinky play, although what they're used for is beyond me.

To a single lady like myself, polyamory sounds terribly exotic and perhaps even sinful. To shed further light on this unique lifestyle, I was able to gain an interview with a dominant known as Sir Sultan Stud. I conducted the interview in my guise as Mistress Dominique, one of the first times I adopted this role. At the time, I hadn't thought of an appropriate costume for my alter ego so I hurriedly put on black leggings along with a misguided birthday present from my nephew Larry: a white t-shirt with "HOT STUFF" written across the front in sparkly red letters. Needless to say, I was quite nervous that day and gave my antiperspirant quite a workout.

Sir Sultan Stud had five women in what he called his **harem**, which he brought along to the interview. It surprised me that they weren't dressed in gauzy veils, as one might expect harem girls to do. Instead, they wore jeans, dirty sneakers and t-shirts emblazoned with the logos of various beer manufacturers. Sir Sultan Stud himself wore bib overalls with no shirt, forcing me to stare at the mass of chest hair peeking out from underneath the bib.

Mistress Dominique: Greetings, Sir Sultan Stud. I see you have the entire harem with you today.

Sir Sultan Stud: Yes, indeed. I'm very proud of our little group. As you can see, all my women are perfectly happy sitting here at my feet and waiting for my next command.

Jasdeep: Why don't you command yourself to buy us new clothes, cheapskate?

Sultan: What? Who said that? Speak up!

Anbumani: And while you're at it, I wouldn't mind a better place to live. Six people in one room at the Route 16 Motel, stinks.

Sultan: All right! That was you, Sultana! I know that voice!

Sultana: It wasn't me. Maybe it was Indira.

Indira: Wasn't me, either. It was Rahneesh.

Rahneesh: For the last time, my name isn't Rahneesh! My parents named me Esther, dammit!

Sultan: I said your name was Rahneesh and that's it! Now be quiet!

Rahneesh: Bite me! Your name is really Greg Haffermeyer—I saw it on your driver's license! Sultan, my ass!

Mistress Dominique: Um, if we could get back on track…?

Jasdeep: I'm hungry. You're taking us out to eat tonight and it's not going to be some dump like the Eddie's Food Trough. I want a real restaurant.

Sultan: Be quiet! All of you!

Indira: What's the matter with the Eddie's Food Trough? They have a great salad bar.

Sultana: That's great if you're a rabbit. I want a steak that doesn't look it came from the hind end of a Golden Retriever.

Sultan: I am your Sultan! I command you all to shut up!

MD: Perhaps we should try this interview at another time…

Rahneesh: Hey, Greggie, what about those new clothes, huh? You gonna cough up some new duds or what?

Sultan: The next person who speaks will receive a whipping!

Anbumani: Last time you did that, the people in the next room called the cops, remember?

Indira: Every day it's the same thing. I should have stayed with my husband back in Paducah.

MD: Well, thank you Sir Sultan Stud and your lovely harem. I think we have at least a little better idea of how a polygamous relationship works.

Sultana: I'm not kidding, either. No more Eddie's Food Trough!

We begin to see that a kinky relationship is complex and difficult to maintain. And yet, Sir Sultan Stud's harem arrangement is only the tip of the iceberg. Kinky people are capable of amazingly complicated relationships that are not for the faint of heart. Be warned, as we continue our journey—the road ahead is bumpy and paved with weirdness.

Chapter Two

The murky world from whence it all came

A BRIEF OVERVIEW OF KINK HISTORY

Do we know how kinky practices began? Do we know who the first kinky people were? Well, no. How about the first kinky sex device? Or the first person to enjoy a good spanking? Unfortunately, no again. The whole thing is quite disappointing when you get down to it. Nevertheless, we shall plunge ahead into the past, using what facts we have to make informed assumptions on how we traveled the slippery slope from there to here.

Prehistoric kink: The earliest known mentions of kink are found in the caves in Vallon Pont-d'Arc, France. This vast underground network of caves is decorated with paintings and engravings dating from the Paleolithic age, some 17,000 to 20,000 years ago. Most of the cave drawings are the usual humdrum stuff: a man armed with a spear battling a dinosaur, a pterodactyl carrying off a baby, and what looks like a spaceman giving an unfortunate person an anal probe.

What interests us are drawings found in one of the smaller caverns, in which a woman dressed in what appears to be black buffalo leather wields a whip while a man wearing a diaper made from leaves and bark cringes at her feet. When these drawings were examined under a magnifying glass, they indicate that the man is wetting himself.

There are also drawings of large, hairy men clubbing other men (or possibly women—the artist wasn't very good) with a cudgel. Obviously, this is one of the first recorded instances of spanking, although it does appear to be harsh. We must remember that paddles hadn't been invented yet, so our earliest ancestors had to make do with what they had.

One more drawing merits attention. It features a man sitting with a bowl turned upside-down on his head. Is this an ancient rite or is it evidence of **sploshing**, a kink that involves people rolling around naked in various food substances? We may never know.

The Egyptians: Unfortunately for the historian, the few surviving cave drawings are the only evidence we have of early kink. In fact, there is a huge blank spot in kink history until the reign of Ramses II, ruler of Egypt from 1285-1218 BC. Considered one of the finest of the numerous Egyptian pharaohs, Ramses II is probably best known as the pharaoh who got into a fight with Yul Brynner and caused all those plagues and other horrible things in that Charlton Heston movie. When he wasn't busy with the plagues and whatnot, Ramses found the time to have eighteen wives and father at least one hundred children. This led him to invent the condom that bears his name to this day. (One of Uncle Henry's desk drawers was full of empty Ramses condom packages. I have no idea what he did with them by himself in the den.)

Of more importance to us, of course, is Ramses' kinky side, which didn't come to light until 1982, when J. Frank Mercer, an Egyptologist, uncovered a previously unexplored chamber in the great Temple of Amon at Karnack. Strange hieroglyphics found in the chamber proved to be quite exciting to scholars, who rushed to the site in droves. Unfortunately, he fixated on the hieroglyphics showing the usual stuff about space aliens building pyramids, along with some babble about Egyptians having the use of D-cell batteries, radio and five-speed blenders. Mercer and his colleagues completely overlooked the compelling evidence that Ramses II and many of his subjects were quite the kinky bunch. Perhaps they found this aspect of Egyptian life embarrassing. Perhaps they were crummy Egyptologists. Regardless, it's been left to other researchers, such as your author, to bring this new and exciting information to the light of day.

The hieroglyphs tell us the Egyptians were very much into bondage, particularly **mummification**. The pharaohs seem to have been particularly fond of this kink, as we can see by looking at any Egyptian structure—there are literally thousands of little mummy drawings carved into them all. In fact, every time one of their tombs is discovered, they find a pharaoh mummified to the point where they couldn't move a muscle.

We know from studying these mummies, that the Egyptians took their bondage seriously, perhaps too seriously. It appears that when they had someone helplessly mummified, they stuck a hook up the person's nose and pulled their brain out, resulting, of course, in the death of victim. Hard core play, indeed.

In addition to bondage, the ancient Egyptians were quite fond of **animal play**, although not the type most familiar to kinksters today, which often features people dressed up as ponies, puppies or badgers. Instead, the Egyptians favored dressing up as birds and dogs. Their symbol for animal play was *Anubis,* most often depicted in hieroglyphs as a man wearing a dog or bird helmet of some sort. We don't know for sure if the people wearing the animal hats were considered dominant or submissive, but there are numerous examples of a dog- or birdman leaning over a mummified person with one of those brain hooks, so it seems safe to assume that they took the dominant role.

Before we leave the land of mummies, pyramids and brain hooks, I must mention Cleopatra, the queen of Egypt and the world's first great **dominatrix**. In a time when most women went around wearing baggy dresses and stringy hair, Cleopatra stood out. Her trademark look, featuring slutty makeup and Cher-like bangs, got many Egyptian men quite hot and bothered. One wonders if Cleopatra was an influence on Tammy Faye Bakker. Remember her? She must spend huge amounts of money on eyeliner. I tried it once and accidentally poked myself in the eye. Never again.

Anyway, one of the men who panted after Cleopatra was a Roman general named Marc Anthony, who became so enraptured with the idea of being Cleopatra's sex slave that he set fire to Rome just to impress her. (We learned earlier that Roman generals were kinky and quite fond of discipline. Obviously Marc went against the grain on this one, making him extra kinky.)

Cleo raised an eyebrow at Anthony's antics but otherwise looked indifferent, so Marc stabbed Julius Caesar. When that failed to get a reaction from his love, he set loose hundreds of lions in the Coliseum, hoping they would eat any Christians who happened to be on the daily tours of the place.

Apparently, this did the trick. Cleopatra ordered a few slaves to roll her up in a carpet and throw her on the floor at Marc's feet. Watching Cleo tumble out of the rug got Marc quite hot. He became even hotter when he saw it was a really nice rug. Apparently, he had a carpet fetish or something.

After that, Marc and Cleopatra sailed away on a boat. Cleo then killed herself with a snake of some sort, probably a diamondback rattler, and the whole thing ended up in misery. The key thing to remember about this is that while Egyptians and Romans were kinky, they didn't always make a lot of sense.

Atlantis: This peculiar island civilization, located near the Pillars of Hercules in the Atlantic Ocean, was first described in the records of Egyptian priests. Unfortunately, since the priests were busy drawing little pictures of mummies, cats and birds on every flat surface they could find, they managed to gloss over Atlantis' rich history.

It was left to the famed Greek philosopher, Plato, writing some two hundred years later, to bring out the torrid details of these kinky islanders. Of course, the Greeks were quite the randy bunch themselves. "Anything goes!" was their motto and they lived up to it. It's amazing that Plato, Aristotle and Socrates got any philosophizing done at all, what with all the lewd and lascivious behavior going on. They'd be sitting on some marble steps, going on and on about politics, the meaning of life and other deep subjects, and suddenly they'd be surrounded by hordes of kinky frolickers, moaning and grunting for all they were worth. Take it from me, it's hard to think clearly with that sort of thing going on.

What makes Atlantis so interesting is that its people built a utopian society and then mysteriously disappeared. One day it was there, then poof! Gone without a trace. Most of what we currently know about Atlantis comes from the German historian/archeologist, Ludwig von Schwein. His views are significant because they oppose the prevailing theory that Atlantis was destroyed by a volcano. Instead, von Schwein posits that kinky technology ended the Atlantian Empire.

As it turns out, kinky behavior was the norm in Atlantis, with the society evenly split between dominants and submissives. While ancient Romans enjoyed frolicking in their public baths, the Atlantians built hundreds of public dungeons filled with bondage devices of ever-increasing size and sophistication. Those few fortunate enough to visit the island marveled at the constant sound of cracking whips and the moans of the submissive victims.

This fervor, this dedication to kink, led to Atlantis' downfall, for not only did the Atlantians have the technology to build intricate kinky devices, they possessed a strange compulsion to make these devices increasingly large. The trouble began when a village on the northern tip of the island became especially popular as a vacation destination. Originally home to a few small community dungeons, the area's popularity caused the rapid construction of larger and larger dungeons, some of them twenty stories tall, according to von Schwein. Within a short time, the area became overcrowded with visiting kinksters and the original dungeons were torn down, replaced by resplendent palaces of kinkiness that soared into the sky.

I can't help but notice at this point that the story begins to sound eerily like the development of Las Vegas. My cousin Merle used to love going out there years ago, to frequent the smaller and older casinos. He became furious when developers tore them down to build newer and bigger ones. "It's like a damned theme park!" he rages. "What happened to the frickin' sin?" So far, Las Vegas hasn't disappeared as Atlantis did but I'll bet cousin Merle would be quite happy to see it go.

Anyway, back in Atlantis, years passed and the northern part of the island continued to draw increasing numbers of happy perverts. The second generation of towering dungeons was replaced by a third generation of truly massive edifices, larger than many of today's domed stadiums. Finally, the island's delicate balance could take no more as the sheer weight of the buildings and people on the northern part of the island caused it to tip on one end. Those who weren't immediately drowned raced uphill for the center of Atlantis, in the hope of restoring the balance. But it was too little, too late, and the whole thing slid quietly into the ocean.

Today, a few crumbling dungeons remain perched on the ocean floor, where they are often mistaken for sunken cathedrals. As von Schwein points out, this belief is easily disproved by looking at the intricately carved walls of these structures, which feature a design of whips intertwined with primitive handcuffs. In addition, ancient stone bondage tables can still be seen, holding the skeletons of their final victims, all of them grinning.

We may never know the entire history of Atlantis. What little remains at the bottom of the ocean stands in mute testimony to a race of proud and naughty people, their majestic creations now home to fish and barnacles and octopuses.

The Chinese: Certainly, lots of kinky things happened after the Atlantians faded from the scene but these are either lost in the mists of time or just aren't that much fun to write about. We move ahead, then, to the history of China. Of particular interest to the kinky historian (meaning a historian interested in kink, and not a historian who is kinky) are the significant inventions of this culture. We all know that the Chinese invented such things as fireworks, ink and takeout restaurants, but less known is the fact that the Chinese invented the **foot fetish**. (Fetishes of all kinds are discussed in much more detail in Chapter Five. I mention this here so you won't think I'm slacking off in this chapter.)

Foot fetishists—the vast majority are men—are a common sight on the Internet these days. Like other fetishists, they derive a great deal of sexual pleasure from a particular object, in this case, feet. Some foot fetishists look for a woman to stomp on them while wearing exotic shoes, while others just want to lick a woman's toes. (Ick. Can you say, bacteria festival?)

And then there are those who obtain their jollies from painting a woman's toenails and others still who like to be kicked by barefooted women. You get the idea. These determined souls are but the latest in a long line of foot freaks who trace their kinky lineage to ancient China, particularly the Song dynasty, which ruled until the thirteenth century when some other dynasty took over.

The people of the Song dynasty, when they weren't busy singing, were absolutely obsessed with feet. No one knows why. Perhaps the constant singing drove everyone crazy. It was a long time ago. At any rate, the fetish with feet first manifested itself with the invention of **high heels**. Unfortunately, unlike today's high heels, the Chinese got the idea a little mixed up and put the heel at the front of the shoe, sort of like an extreme Earth Shoe. (For those who weren't around in the 1970s, the heel of the Earth Shoe was lower than the toes. For a few years, they were quite popular until people realized how ugly they were and threw them out.)

The backward high heel turned out to be an incredibly stupid idea, as the wearer required assistance just to stand, at which point they would pitch backward and smash the back of their heads on the floor. Chinese records recently uncovered by a team of archeologists reveal that nearly 450,000 deaths occurred as a result of wearing these shoes before Chinese shoe designers reluctantly gave up on the idea.

Following this debacle, the foot fetish took a new form. Perhaps frustrated by the failure of the high heel thing, it became popular in Chinese culture to bind the feet of particularly attractive young girls with strips of cloth. This foot bondage went on until the girl grew to womanhood, at which point the cloth was removed, revealing seriously deformed and ugly feet. Bystanders immediately clamored for the cloth to be put back on, and not only because the feet were ugly—they *really* stunk, enough to bring tears to your eyes and there was no help from Dr. Scholl, who had yet to be born. Nevertheless, these tiny-footed women became the object of intense sexual fantasies by Chinese men, spawning a subculture of foot fetishists who couldn't get enough of tiny tootsies.

As time went on, an entire sex industry arose to support the foot fetishists. *Koneechi-Was,* as the women who endured the foot-binding called themselves, found a steady market for their tiny shoes. In fact, demand far outstripped the supply. Desperate foot fetishists, lacking a forum such as the Internet, resorted to scrawling their desires for the shoes on the walls of the *Koneechi-Was'* homes. While most fetishists were content to own any pair of tiny shoes, there remained a fanatical group more focused in their kinky desires, demanding shoes that were especially odoriferous. They often attacked *Koneechi-Was* as they hobbled along the street, knocking them down and stealing their footwear. (There is an oddly similar kink popular today in the market for smelly women's underwear and socks. For more information, see Chapter Five, Fetishes.)

The craze for miniature used footwear eventually petered out, much to the relief of millions of Chinese girls who didn't have to suffer the torment of foot binding. Newer kinks emerged that caught the kinky public's attention, many of them involving chopsticks and interesting places to put them.

The Vikings: For a three hundred year period beginning in 800 AD, a group of Scandinavian kinksters based in Sweden roamed the ocean, from time to time making land and slaughtering whatever local people they found. Occasionally, a few local denizens would escape death only to become the Vikings' slaves, spending the rest of their years in forced labor. These slaves rowed the large boats the Vikings used to get from place to place on their killing and looting sprees, pulling their oars to a relentless rhythm pounded out on a drum by a large woman wearing a helmet with horns sticking out of each side. The woman accompanied her drum pounding by singing *arias,* a Viking word roughly analogous to the English word *disco*. At any rate, the beat was the important thing and those unfortunates who didn't keep up the pace were beaten by whip-wielding dominants, something that caused major problems when the rowing crew was comprised of masochists, who tended to do little rowing and a lot of happy screaming.

Those slaves not utilized as rowers were set to work in the vast Viking sex toy factories in Schleswig-Holstein, Sweden. Some factories specialized in iron restraints such as manacles, chastity belts and collars. Other production facilities took advantage of the Vikings' skill in creating sex toys of excellent quality. These included dildos, butt plugs and ball gags made from walrus tusks, canes and other striking implements created from reindeer antlers, and a line of fetish clothing made from the pelts of whatever animals happened to get in their way.

Yes, despite their violent nature, the Vikings were a creative people. I'm not much of a sports fan but evidently they also created professional football. I know from looking at the sports page that at least one of their football teams still survives. I believe it's in North Dakota or Minnesota.

The kinky Vikings didn't stop at sex toys. Today's vast Swedish pornographic industry got its start when the Vikings created what they euphemistically referred to as "Icelandic Sagas," which were actually torrid porn carved on large rocks, or *Runes*. Lacking the ability to make paper, the Vikings carved all of their "sagas" on these Runes, with some of the juicier tales requiring rocks so large they had to be carried by several men. Apparently, the most popular of the naughty novelists of the Viking era was a man named Leif Eriksson, whose name shows up on quite a few of the surviving randy rocks.

Carving spicy tales on huge stones made privacy impossible, resulting in a society where pornography was freely read and discussed in open society. Many Viking hamlets built large arenas where town criers yelled out the latest sexy saga to a packed house of groaning, grappling villagers. This tradition is carried on today by Swedish television, where nearly everyone is naked and does whatever they please, at least according to my neighbor Edwin, who has a cousin in Sweden or Norway.

The sexual violence of Viking culture is clearly evident in the character of Thor, the most famous of all Vikings. Thor was one of the first practitioners of **edge play**, an activity in which a dominant encourages a submissive to stretch their kinky boundaries. Due to Thor's extreme attachment to Odin, the name he gave his favorite hammer, his idea of edge play was to induce his subs to lie still while he smashed them repeatedly. There is little historical detail as to why he did this but one Rune contains an account claiming Thor killed hundreds of people in his lifetime, so he obviously liked rough sex a lot. He probably wasn't too popular at Viking sex clubs, I would imagine.

The Middle Ages: This era, spanning roughly 500 to 1500 AD, is marked by great upheaval, especially following the decline and fall of the Roman Empire. Certainly, lots of events took place in the Middle Ages but our interest concerns the various popes, emperors, barons and kings who popped up all over the place, especially in Europe.

These men of power, no matter what kingdom they ruled over, seemed to have a common desire to erect large castles. (Yes, it's the same penis compensation business practiced by contemporary men who drive those gigantic SUVs. Some things never change.) And what do we find in the basements of these castles? Vast dungeons that's what, containing all the latest gadgets for inflicting torment. These parlors of pain were so well designed were that contemporary dungeons are little changed from those created in the Middle Ages.

England seems to have embraced dungeons more than any other European nation. Even today, you can tour dozens of ancient castles to see for yourself what a medieval dungeon looks like. I recently visited a typical medieval fortress, Shiresmatheringham Castle, located in the Northumberland part of England. (Sadly, the trip to the United Kingdom took all my frequent flyer miles. Because of that, I was unable to travel to Hawaii and investigate reports of kinky behavior among the ancient Hawaiian people involving cheap flowered shirts and macadamia nuts. Oh, well. Perhaps I'll make it there before the second edition of this research is published.)

Getting to back to our dungeon, Smatherington is currently home to Sir Oswald Fork-Smithinghamshire, twelfth earl of Worcestershireham or some such thing. These people insist on long, convoluted names and it's hard to keep them straight. Unfortunately, I didn't have an opportunity to meet Mr. Fork or whatever he calls himself, so I don't know if he's a kinkster or not.

Of course, my tour of the castle included a fascinating visit to the ancestral dungeon, maintained much the way it appeared when it was first created in 876 AD. It's a kinkster's delight, to say the least! The dank, low-ceiled torture chamber flickered eerily in the weak yellow light coming from torches mounted in narrow slits in the thick stone walls. These walls, under close examination, reveal messages carved in desperation by long ago victims. "If I must die, I beg it be done quickly," reads one heartrending scrawl, signed by a man known only as Anthony. In a dark corner is another note: "Here I sit, broken-harted [sic], Came for pain and only pharted."

The dungeon includes many devices used by contemporary kinksters, including a bed of nails, a chair covered in iron spikes, leg and arm irons, thumb screws, iron cages both large and small, a fireplace stocked with branding irons, and, perhaps most menacing of all, the Iron Maiden. Standing as tall as a man, its case painted with the placid face of the Iron Maiden herself, this hideous contraption opens on ancient, creaky hinges to reveal hundreds of sharp spikes, waiting to impale the next unfortunate soul when the case is closed on them.

As I stood pondering the dungeon's collection of torture devices, an Australian man walked up next to me and began whimpering as he lovingly caressed a set of iron restraints bolted to a wall. Watching him, I felt the cold presence of all the victims who suffered in this horrific place, as though the stone walls spoke to me of tragedy and horror. The feelings grew and I knew I was on the verge of absorbing the true meaning of all that went on there. But the Australian man chose that moment to unzip his pants and fondle himself, moaning loudly. When he began rubbing against me, I yelled for help. By the time the castle security guards hustled him away, my moment of intuition had passed.

On my way out of the dungeon, I nearly tripped on a trapdoor set into the floor. Looking through its small, barred window, I saw what appeared to be the bones of some long-forgotten sufferer curled in the corner of a cramped cell. That's when the full impact of medieval kink hit home. Like the Egyptians and their brain hooks, the people of Shiresmatheringham castle were hardcore players. I saw, in my mind's eye, a leather-clad king, laughing with glee as he tortured an unfortunate submissive on the rack. I heard the crackle of the fire as the branding iron grew red-hot in the fireplace. And then that Australian man broke free and ran back into the dungeon, screeching as he threw himself on the bed of nails. His screams of agony and massive blood loss broke my reverie and even though the tour wasn't finished, I gave no resistance as the guards hurried our tour group out of the castle. An ambulance screamed past our bus as we left the grounds.

The Renaissance: If the Vikings had paper, they could have read their pornography in private, saving many men from hernias caused by carrying those Runes around. Perhaps Vikings just liked to show off; historians believe the Chinese invented paper some 700 years before the rise of Viking culture. It might not have done much good anyway, as paper was very expensive and all books were hand-copied by monks utilizing quill pens.

As a result, books were scarce and tended to be religious texts, which wouldn't have interested a Viking looking for the latest adventures of "Naughty Helga" or whatever they titled their "sagas". Even the monks creating religious tomes sometimes found their work tedious. To alleviate their boredom, they inserted strange passages in the books to see if anyone really paid attention. One such passage, snuck in a religious text recounting the spread of Christianity, made a jibe at the expense of the Grand Duke of Moscow, Ivan III, better known as Ivan the Great. Translated from the original Latin, it reads, "Ivan the third; does it with birds." Rather juvenile, don't you think?

So, what does this mean to kinksters? Quite a bit, actually, because the books created by mischievous monks signaled the end of the Middle Ages and the dawn of the Renaissance, with its great innovations in art, science and literature. The Renaissance saw not only a dramatic increase in paper production but also a major technological innovation that rocked the world, one that made kinky materials available to nearly everyone.

I refer, of course, to Germany's Johan Gutenberg, who invented the printing press in 1485. For the first time, books could be produced in great quantity and distributed far and wide. Unfortunately, very few people knew how to read, so Gutenberg nearly went bankrupt as his storeroom filled with unsold books. He saved his foundling publishing business when he came up with the idea of picture books, which didn't require reading ability. His first efforts were rather pedestrian—crude drawings of houses, farm animals and Herr Barkheimer, the Gutenberg family dog. These books weren't popular, mainly because Gutenberg was a terrible artist. His rendition of Herr Barkheimer was so awful that many people thought it to be a drawing of a demon coming to steal their souls. They threw the books into the fire to save themselves, then spread the word not to buy anything printed by Gutenberg.

Things looked bleak until Gutenberg had a moment of inspiration that not only solved his problem but also got the Renaissance off to a roaring start and simultaneously created of the pornography industry as we know it today. It came about when Gutenberg decided to hire established artists to create the picture books. After a friend told him some pretty hot stuff was going on in Italy, Gutenberg promptly offered several of the better-known Italian artists the opportunity to make some extra money drawing simple pictures. Soon, he began receiving large packages of art from such names as da Vinci, Michelangelo, Botticelli, Raphael and Titian. (Historians are pretty sure this last name was actually the punch line to a Renaissance joke and not a real person.)

To Gutenberg's amazement, the packages contained beautifully drawn smut. As it turned out, his Italian was none too good and the letters he sent to the Italian artists asked them not for nature studies as he intended, but for "the really hot stuff, if you know what I mean." The Italians shrugged, decided it was easy money and supplied Gutenberg with some of the finest pornography ever seen.

Gutenberg was at first reluctant to publish his newly acquired collection of porn but he had spent the last of his money paying the artists and had no choice. He arranged the drawings in a way he thought would tell the story of men and women enjoying the beauty of nature. Unfortunately, Gutenberg was ever the frustrated artist and couldn't resist embellishing the drawings. His crude additions, especially the inclusion of Herr Barkheimer in several scenes, turned the collection into something resembling an orgy, complete with a myriad of sex devices. The resulting book, "Nature Studies of People Not Wearing Clothes," became an instant hit with Renaissance perverts, forcing Gutenberg back to his press time and time again to produce enough copies to meet the demand.

Gutenberg made so much money from the smut book that he was able to print inexpensive copies of the Bible, which he gave away to anyone who asked. Unfortunately, due to the thickness of the paper he used, his Bible was darned near as big as a Rune and required several burly men and/or women to carry it. A series of accidents involving these enormous tomes resulted in lawsuits that finally drove Gutenberg out of business, a sad end to a remarkable story.

The Aztecs: As the Renaissance took hold in Europe, a quite different civilization began its ascent in South America, particularly in the area now known as Mexico. It was the dawn of the Aztecs, a kinky bunch who created a mighty empire stretching from ocean to ocean. Aztec culture and politics were based on competition between the various city-states that comprised the empire, ruled by the great warrior, Montezuma. As far as I can tell, Montezuma must have been some sort of Typhoid Mary. Even today, visitors to Mexico speak of catching a terrible affliction known as "Montezuma's revenge," which apparently causes violent, unrelenting bowel movements. Sounds awful.

Interestingly, the Aztecs developed their kink in ways similar to the Egyptians. For example, men often dressed as birds, probably to engage in animal play. Unlike the Egyptians, I suspect Aztec birdmen were submissives, subject to the commands of their dominant trainers, who may have taught them to perch in cages, whistle happy little tunes and nibble at cuttlefish, which I believe are common activities involved in that sort of thing.

The Aztecs also built pyramids much like those in Egypt but with a significant difference—Aztec pyramids featured thousands of steps on all four sides. Some researchers theorize these steps represent a form of extreme aerobic exercise but it's more likely they served a kinkier purpose. Large stone slabs rested at the top of the stairs and surviving picture writing tells us these slabs were used for extreme pain play, similar to the Egyptians and their brain hooks.

As far as we can tell, a typical Aztec kinky scene involved dragging a bound submissive up all those steps and then plopping them on the stone slab. A dominant dressed as a bird or puma or whatever would then repeatedly stab the submissive and yank out their still-beating heart. This caused great rejoicing by the other dominants gathered nearby, who would begin a ritual dance until one of the dominants fell off the top of the pyramid and down all those stairs. Of course, by the time the dominant reached bottom, they'd broken every bone in their body and were either dead or wishing they were. This, in turn, caused rejoicing among the submissives gathered at the base of the pyramid, none of whom really wanted to get dragged to the top and stabbed in the first place. Unfortunately, the submissives' glee enraged the remaining dominants, who dragged yet another sub up to the stone slab, where the whole terrible cycle repeated itself until no one remained alive.

It's little wonder that Spanish invaders, led by Hernán Cortés, so easily conquered the Aztecs. By the time they arrived, most of the able-bodied men were dead either from having their hearts yanked out or falling off the pyramid. The few men left alive figured that whatever the Spanish wanted to do to them, it couldn't be any worse than that, so they surrendered quickly and shortly afterward got their heads cut off by the Spaniards, who at that time were a rather bloodthirsty lot themselves.

The Canadians: The history of Canada goes back to the year 1534, when French explorer Jacques Cartier got lost while exploring what would become upper Michigan. In fact, Cartier became so lost that he left the future Michigan and strayed into a new country. Prior to this, many in pre-America were unaware that anything of note existed to the north; others knew there was something up there but assumed it was uninhabitable by humans and didn't think about it very often. Oddly enough, this is still largely the case today, as I discovered when I once quizzed my nephew, Dewey, about Canada. He said he'd been taught in school that Canada was home to many polar bears and that it snowed every day of the year. He couldn't remember anything else worth mentioning.

Unlike Dewey, Jacques Cartier found the new country quite exciting, gleefully naming it Canada, from the Eskimo word *canuck*, which I'm told means, "I'm damned sick of all this snow and that polar bear tried to eat me." Sadly, before Cartier could interest anyone else in his great discovery, a polar bear ate the explorer and Canada was soon forgotten.

In 1829, many Americans became aware of Canada for the first time when thousands of Canadians, fed up with the cold, snow and polar bears, immigrated to the south, most of them settling in the still-untamed American West. It is here that their kinky proclivities first gained notice. Adopting such titles as "Wild Bill" and "Pecos Pete," Canadian dominants began practicing their craft and soon attracted throngs of adoring submissives. Armed with such bondage devices as branding irons, barbed wire and rope lariats, the Canadians soon developed a style of BDSM that fit nicely with their new environment.

Oddly enough, most of the Canadian kinksters were compulsive exhibitionists. Fearful of retribution for their sexual proclivities and yet compelled to perform in public, they compromised by creating the rodeo. On the surface, rodeos seem like a harmless demonstration of the skills needed by a cowboy; in truth, they are barely disguised exhibitions of kink utilizing animals instead of humans. I mean, come on! Rodeos are full of ropes and leather pants and harnesses and people with weird names like "Dutch" and "Wrangler Sue." It's time for these people to come out of the closet, don't you think?

Anyway, the kinky Canucks didn't stop with rodeos. They also frequented the saloons and bordellos found in every western town, most of them equipped with a back room where all manner of deviant practices went on. **Ponyplay**, of course, was very popular, with dominants saddling their submissives and riding them around the room while trying not to get bucked off. (See Chapter Six, Lifestyles, for an account of my own experience as a ponygirl.)

The backroom crowd especially enjoyed calf roping, which gave the dominants ample opportunity to use their ubiquitous lariats as they competed to see who could tie up a submissive in the fastest time. Bullwhips were also in evidence, with competitions held to see who could make a sub jump the furthest or who could create the most pleasing welt design on a victim's back. Some of the more skilled whip artists even played games of tic-tac-toe on their submissives' buttocks.

Today, the kinky Canadian heritage continues to be popular, as seen in the growing number of rodeos. There is even a professional rodeo organization whose members tour the country, competing for increasingly large amounts of prize money. The winning dominant also receives a gigantic belt buckle, usually decorated with some sort of kinky activity. In recent years, "junior rodeos" have been established for younger Canadians, thus ensuring yet another generation will continue the tradition of exhibitionist kink that hints at the even kinkier stuff going on behind closed doors.

The civilizations described in this chapter are but a few of the kinky cultures that have thrived throughout history. Indeed, a more inclusive history would require several volumes all to itself. It is hoped that you will get at least a taste of kinky practices throughout the ages and come to the understanding that today's kinky crowd is but the latest in a line of pervs stretching back to the dawn of mankind itself. Perhaps you will see history in a different way, knowing what you now know. You may find yourself wondering about noted historical figures, as I often do. What did Benjamin Franklin do when Thomas Jefferson and his other friends weren't around? And what about the Spanish Inquisition—was it as innocent as it seems? How about the Portuguese? Are they as innocent as they seem? Or that one pope, the one nobody wants to talk about. What was he up to? The answers are there, if only you look hard enough.

Chapter Three

Toys for kinky girls and boys—It's not just whips and chains anymore.

TOYS THROUGHOUT HISTORY

What would a kinky person be without their toys? Yes, I said toys but not the kind Santa puts under a youngster's tree. Quite the contrary! When kinksters talk about toys, they usually refer to devices that either render a person immobile, cause them a great deal of pain or both. It's hard for some of us to look at a vicious flogger or a set of restraints used to hang someone upside-down and think of them as toys but kinky people do. Go figure.

In order to understand your average kinkster and what they do with their toys from the dark side, we need to look back in history to see the development of these devices and the interesting people responsible for them.

Toymaster: In Chapter One we met the Marquis de Sadist, the man generally credited with inventing sadistic behavior. Unfortunately, history has overlooked the Marquis' brother-in-law, Earl, who plays an equally significant role in shaping kinky conduct in contemporary society. Historical research shows us it was Earl, though his ceaseless experimentation, who invented many of the more popular implements used by dominants on their submissives. Unlike the Marquis, who amused himself throwing things at people in the hopes of causing them pain, Earl de Sadist was a truly bent twig who brought technology to the dungeon.

What made Earl so evil was his combination of sheer depravity and brilliant creativity. Like most great inventors, he started small, contenting himself by sneaking up behind people and giving them a painful "wedgie". But what is a wedgie? According to my nephew Ralphie, whom I consider to be a typical teenager, young men are apparently fond of going up to other young men, grabbing the waistband of the victim's underwear and pulling upward with a great deal of force, thus producing the wedgie. It sounds horrible but then young men tend to do horrible things and no one has been able to figure out how to stop them. Interestingly, in Canada wedgies are punishable by law, as in the case of R. vs. Engfield (Ontario Judgments: [1991] O.J. No. 1226) in which a young man who administered a wedgie was found guilty of assault and thrown in jail. I shall have to tell Ralphie of this, lest he get any ideas.

Okay, I've gotten completely off the track, so let's get back to Earl, who had run into a roadblock in his desire to administer wedgies. As it turns out, underpants didn't exist in the 18th century and without underpants, the whole wedgie business becomes a problem. But Earl put his genius to work, inventing underwear in both boxer and brief styles. He then spent a fortune building hundreds of shops to sell the new undergarments and another fortune hiring town criers to advertise his wares. Luckily for Earl, underwear proved to be extremely popular with the public. Not only did he make back his investment plus a lot more, he had created thousands of underpants-wearing victims, allowing him to deliver wedgies to his heart's content.

Earl de Sadist's pioneering efforts didn't stop there. When the thrill of wedgies faded, he put his great brain to work and after months of painstaking experimentation, he emerged from his workshop with a revolutionary kinky invention: the nipple clamp.

This device, as we know it today, is an insidious teethed gadget that fastens tightly on the nipple, resulting in extreme pain for the victim. If you were to examine a standard nipple clamp, you would find it resembles a pair of tiny alligator jaws and with good reason—Earl's first nipple clamps were a pair of live baby alligators trained to bite nipples on sight.

At first, this innovation thrilled Earl and his kinky pals, so much so that Earl started an alligator farm on the de Sadist estates. Before long, he had enough baby alligators to imperil every nipple for miles around but a problem soon arose when the cute baby alligators matured into vicious adult beasts. This dilemma became apparent one fateful day when Earl used mature alligators on one of his submissives, only to watch in horror as the creature ripped off the woman's head and swallowed it whole. After this unfortunate event occurred several more times, Earl went back to his workshop, toiling for several months until he hit upon the idea of making the nipple clamps out of metal, thus giving birth to the device as we know it today.

Another of Earl's devious inspirations came during a tour of Germany, when he stopped for lunch at a tavern in the small hamlet of Wartenburg. While munching on his favorite dish, baby quails in a white wine sauce, Earl happened to glance out of a window to see a young woman run down by a wagon, its wheels crushing her to death.

Being a sadist of the first order, Earl was nearly overcome with glee at the idea of using a wheel to inflict pain on his submissives. Emulating Archimedes, he stood and shouted "Eureka!" at his fellow diners, causing many of them to spill their bowls of schortzengruben or whatever foul thing they were eating.

I should mention here it was no accident that Earl borrowed Archimedes' famous exclamation. In addition to being the greatest mathematician of ancient times,

Archimedes was a bit of a perv himself. As the story goes, he liked to work out complicated math problems while soaking in the tub but on one particular day his efforts to solve an especially tricky theorem resulted only in frustration. He had nearly given up when the answer suddenly came to him. "Eureka!" he shouted, jumping out of the tub. Unfortunately, he then decided to share his excitement with the neighbors and ran stark naked out the front door and down the village street, screaming his head off. Even worse, he enjoyed the experience so much he decided to do all his theorizing in the buff and became a common sight, running starkers around town yelling at the top of his lungs. He was finally thrown in jail by disgusted townspeople who had tired of their children watching in horror as Archimedes made another of his nude dashes.

Happily, back in Wartenburg, Earl de Sadist only borrowed Archimedes catchphrase and not his habit of streaking. After shouting "Eureka!" he excitedly described his latest flash of inspiration to the man seated at the next table. Unfortunately, that man was a Pakistani merchant who had no idea what Earl said and simply nodded and smiled.

That was all the approval Earl needed. He eagerly set about sketching his newest torture device, a giant wheel rolling on hundreds of sharp spikes mounted around the rim. With a wild gleam in his eye, Earl waved the drawing at the patrons of the inn and announced the invention of the Gutenberg Wheel. The name was changed a few minutes later when Earl's coachman informed him that they were, in fact, in Cologne. Earl promptly stood again and announced the Cologne Wheel, but an hour later, a passing minstrel told them they were actually in Hapsburg, so Earl made yet another announcement.

The next day, while preparing to leave, the innkeeper straightened out the whole mess by confirming that Earl and his party were definitely in Wartenburg. After one last announcement, Earl canceled the rest of his European tour and rushed back to the family estates, where he had his team of craftsmen build the world's first Wartenburg Wheel.

It was like nothing seen before. Not satisfied with the relatively small wheels that caused so much pain to the woman run down by the wagon in Wartenburg, Earl had his craftsmen built a monstrous wheel fifteen feet high and two feet across, covered with six inch iron spikes. It weighed nearly half a ton.

Not surprisingly, the first use of the Wartenburg Wheel ended in tragedy. Earl invited Eugenia, one of his favorite mistresses, for a visit and "a bit of fun," as he liked to say. Eugenia, perhaps not the brightest bulb on the tree, allowed Earl to stake her to the road that ran in front of the de Sadist estates. Then Earl signaled his men, standing on top of a nearby hill. Grunting with effort, they managed to push the behemoth wheel down the steep slope. Moving much faster than anyone expected, it rolled unerringly down the road and thundered across Eugenia's midsection.

Most people wouldn't be surprised to learn Eugenia died almost instantly. Unfortunately, Earl was a bit dense in that regard, genuinely startled that his victim had died a horrible death. He retired to his workshop, muttering to himself.

Weeks later, a new wheel emerged, this one utilizing wooden spikes rather than the iron spikes of the first model. Once again, the mighty wheel roared down the hill toward the road where another of Earl's mistresses was staked. The result was the same—a quick but horrible death.

Further refinements in the design of the spikes were no more successful, taking the lives of several more mistresses, a passing concubine and a herd of sheep. After many late nights desperately tinkering in his workshop, Earl decided that a change in material was needed. Weeks later, a gigantic wheel made of stone rumbled down the hill, resulting in the particularly gruesome death of Earl's sister-in-law and a stonemason who inadvertently wandered in the path of the monstrous device.

The solution to the problem arrived in the person of Dolores, Earl's sole surviving mistress. Warily eyeing the giant wheel that Earl wished to use on her as a sexual device, Dolores blurted, "Not bloody likely!" and stomped off to her carriage in a huff. No amount of cajoling would budge her, nor would promises of chocolates and naughty negligées. "The blinkin' thing's too big!" Dolores shouted at Earl. "Make it smaller, you twit!"

Realizing he had pretty much exhausted the available supply of mistresses and horrified at the thought of going anywhere near his wife, who was an extraordinarily ugly woman with a shrieking voice, Earl put his genius to work. After many more late nights in the workshop, he emerged holding a much smaller version of the wheel. The latest incarnation was a spiked metal wheel about the size of a belt buckle you might see at one of those kinky Canadian rodeos, complete with a handle for ease of use.

Dolores, being something of a masochist, loved the new wheel, especially since it posed no threat of mutilating or crushing her. For his part, Earl felt somewhat disappointed that the wheel wasn't more threatening but if it kept Dolores happy and removed any need to sleep with his wife, he was willing to go along with it.

Oddly enough, the medical community has adopted the Wartenburg Wheel for its own use. It's not uncommon for a physician to run the wheel along the bottom of a person's foot or on their hand to test a patient's neurological reflexes. Or at least that's what they want us to think.

Patron Saint: Imagine being strapped to a large wooden cross. You writhe helplessly while the cackles of an evil dominant ring in your ears. Then you feel the first lash of the whip and realize the fiendish device to which you are bound has made much of your helpless body available for torment. That's the idea behind the St. Andrew's cross, a common feature in many contemporary dungeons and playrooms.

Who would invent such a fiendish device? The story begins in the 14th century, when a Scotsman named Andrew O'McTavish traveled through Greece spreading the word of Christianity and trying to get the Greeks to quit eating those awful gyro things. Have you ever tried a gyro? I did once but never again. They're just plain icky. Try tuna salad. Now there's a sandwich!

Anyway, Andrew became a common sight in the Greek countryside, exhorting the virtues of Christianity while bemoaning gyro consumption. "Listen up, Greeks!" Andrew shouted to anyone who would listen. "You must have a balanced diet. Fish is nice. How about a little fish once in a while? You'll probably rot in hell if you keep this up." Andrew's rants went on for months until the Greeks finally ran out of patience and decided he had to go. They hired a couple of Roman hit men, who took Andrew to a secluded spot and hung him on a cross. Hordes of Greeks came to witness Andrew's fate, pelting him with rocks and stale bits of pita bread. Andrew continued to howl about his favorite subjects, Christianity and gyros, but finally he choked to death on a well-thrown rock that lodged in his throat. His last words were a mumbled condemnation of gyros and anything made with olive oil.

Word of Andrew's demise eventually got back to Scotland, where the Scottish people, in a moment of patriotic fervor, redesigned the national flag. At first, the newly designed flag contained the word *Greeks* with a line crossed through it but this addition was quickly dropped as being tacky.

The final flag design consisted of a white cross on a blue field, quite tasteful and well balanced, unlike many flags, which have no sense of color or design at all. Ever see the Albanian flag? It looks like a cat got sick on a black light poster. Yikes!

At any rate, the new Scottish flag made its way to the Vatican and so impressed the Pope that he made Andrew a saint. Today, St. Andrew is the Patron Saint of Scotland, and St. Andrew's Day is celebrated by Scots around the world on November 30th, a holiday that features a great deal of drinking, golfing and vomiting, apparently because St. Andrew invented golf before his unfortunate tour of Greece.

Having written all this, it now seems unclear what St. Andrew had to with the dungeon implement that bears his name. Perhaps Scottish kinksters wanted to pay him homage in their own unique way or it could be that St. Andrew engaged in pervy activities not yet uncovered by historians. I don't know. Judging from the pictures in Uncle Henry's books, the St. Andrew's cross is more like an "X" than a cross, so the whole thing becomes quite confusing.

Well, it just goes to show there is much of history still shrouded in mystery, like that whole kilt business and the Loch Ness monster that ate that Braveheart fellow. If you'd like to read more about St. Andrew, consult the excellent Scottish history text, *Who the Hell Is St. Andrew, Anyway?* by Shamus McO'Shannesy.

The power of electricity: We would be remiss if we didn't recognize the contributions of another kinky innovator, Thomas Edison. No, not *that* Thomas Edison, the man who invented the light bulb, record player and pocket fisherman, but a different Thomas Edison, a kinky one who lived in Bonnie, Illinois during the same time period as his more famous namesake. This unfortunate coincidence is perhaps the reason the kinky Edison's accomplishments have nearly been lost to history.

The pervy Edison's legacy is most obvious in the continued popularity of the device known as The Enormous Nookie Stimulator or TENS unit. Many kinksters enjoy this gizmo, which sends out little electric shocks to the victim, resulting in sexual arousal for some reason. I've shocked myself on the toaster more times than I can remember and not once did I become aroused. I swear, some of this stuff flies right over my head.

Today's TENS units are small boxes utilizing state-of-the-art microelectronics and are easily obtained at any kinky store or website. This was not the case in the early 20th century. The TENS prototype created by Edison (the kinky one, not the Edison in New Jersey inventing electric chairs and whatnot) was a gigantic thing weighing nearly three tons. This was partly due to the technology of the time, which required Edison to use bulky vacuum tubes and massive power generators, and partly due to the fact that Edison had a thing about size. "Build it bigger, boys!" he shouted to his workmen. "Make sure it's noisy, too!" (Men like big, noisy things. How else to explain those Monster Truck shows?)

The first working model of the TENS unit took nearly a year to build and cost over a million dollars. Most of the money to pay for the invention came from James K. Polk—not the former president but a Bonnie man with the same name. (A check of the Bonnie phone book reveals three men named Millard Fillmore, two Calvin Coolidges and four Nikita Kruschevs. What an odd place.) Anyway, Polk thought he had invested in a radish harvesting machine. Needless to say, he became infuriated when he discovered that Edison's creation harvested orgasms rather than radishes. A huge legal battle ensued that carried all the way to the United States Supreme Court, but that's another story.

Edison first tested the TENS equipment in 1924, using Eleanor Roosevelt as his test subject. (Do I need to mention it wasn't the famous Eleanor Roosevelt? I didn't think so.) Eleanor thought she was undergoing experimental treatment to relieve her gout but she should have known better. After all, the table to which she was strapped was dwarfed by the TENS unit, which stood nearly thirty feet tall and required fifteen men to operate. Edison himself wired Eleanor to the machine, with many of the wires terminating in a helmet Edison fashioned from one of his wife's colanders. In all, it took several hours to make all the appropriate connections. Edison took special care with the connections to the subject's sex organs, which probably explains why it took so long.

Finally, with all the preparations made, Edison signaled his men to activate the TENS device. Immediately, a deafening roar filled the room. Vibrations shook the laboratory walls as the air filled with smoke and the acrid smell of ozone. And over the din of the machinery, Eleanor let loose with a hideous scream that made everyone's skin crawl.

"More power!" screamed Edison.

"I canna give you more power!" howled the chief engineer, a man named Scotty. "She's gonna blow any second!"

As the massive TENS unit shook wildly, Eleanor's screams grew louder, piercing the thick smoke and bits of debris filling the lab. Then, just as the engineer predicted, the massive TENS unit exploded. The blast destroyed Edison's laboratory and leveled homes in Bonnie for six square blocks. It caused a number of local pregnant women to go into premature labor. It rattled windows in the nearby towns of Sesser and Ina. (The mayor of Ina, by the way, was a man named Fidel Castro but not *that* Fidel Castro, blah blah blah.) And with World War I still fresh in their minds, local men armed themselves with rifles and pitchforks, convinced that the dreaded Hun had launched a sneak attack on Bonnie. A hastily formed militia unit soon arrived at Edison's lab to take control of the situation.

They found Edison picking his way out of a pile of rubble, babbling incoherently about rheostats and coil windings. Soon afterward, they pulled Eleanor from the wreckage. Unfortunately, she was beyond help but it was impossible not to notice she wore the biggest grin any of them had ever seen.

Edison rebuilt his lab and continued to work on the development of kinky technology. Sadly, his experiments almost always resulted in an explosion of some sort and the townspeople finally drove him out of what little remained of Bonnie. He died in obscurity, shortly after inventing that little thing that makes pinball machines tilt if you push on them too hard.

Smooth move: One of the unsung heroes of kinkdom is Wylie C. Armbrister, inventor of what we know today as personal lubricant. In the late 19th century, Mr. Armbrister owned a chemist's shop in a rather seedy part of London. He was a lifelong bachelor and probably with good reason—he liked nothing better that sticking objects up his butt. Why he did this is not revealed by history. We only know that whenever he could grab a spare moment, Armbrister would dash into the back room of his shop and begin stuffing himself. Bottles, small boxes, broomsticks; he wasn't picky about what he shoved up there.

You're probably thinking this activity sounds painful, not to mention weird. I would imagine so! Leaving the weird aspect aside, we can say with some certainty that Armbrister wasn't much into pain and that his exhaustive experimentation in developing the ideal lubricant was motivated by the desire to relieve the discomfort he felt while engaging in his favorite activity.

It took Armbrister nearly two years to arrive at a formula that suited his needs; a clear, gelatinous substance he proudly named Wylie's Bum Grease. Word of this amazing substance spread quickly amongst London's kinksters and soon Armbrister had a steady business, selling his brightly colored jars to furtive men who tended to arrive at the shop just before closing. In a couple of years Armbrister made so much money from Wylie's Bum Grease that he retired to an estate in the south of England, where he hired Frenchmen to poke at his nether regions with a wide variety of pointy objects.

Armbrister's legacy lives on today in the dozens of personal lubricants on display at drug stores and kink shops around the world. The easy availability of slippery goop has led to a steady increase in the popularity of people sticking things up various bodily orifices. Today's hardcore kinkster would feel ill equipped indeed without a generous supply of lubricant to aid in the insertion of a multitude of devices into their own body cavities or those of others.

As I've learned from my travels, no hole is safe from impalement these days. From what information I've been able to gather, many kinksters are fond of slathering long, thin tubes with lubricant and shoving them up a vicitm's nose or even in the mouth and down into the stomach. This is an important ritual in **medical play**, in which the dominant takes the role of an evil doctor or nurse, while the submissive plays the helpless patient, forced to endure the insertion of various gizmos while wearing one of those awful examination gowns that always leave the buttocks exposed for everyone to see. Whoever invented those things is probably kinky too.

Speaking of buttocks, they remain the most popular point of insertion. Dominants can't get enough of sliding

dildos, tubes of all sizes, **butt plugs**, small mammals and golf clubs up a sub's rear end. Why, you ask? I have no idea. Nor do I have any idea why some kinksters like to insert items, some of them frighteningly large, into the urethra. What happens next is anyone's guess. (My sister Louise looked over my shoulder as I typed this section then she gasped and fled the room. Apparently, she doesn't want to guess.)

Regardless of what Louise might think, it could well be that Wylie C. Armbrister is looking down on all the orifice stuffing, no doubt smiling and nodding in approval.

TODAY'S TOYBOX

If you are new to the kink world, be prepared to get out your checkbook, credit card or a handful of cash because you can't be kinky these days without lots and lots of toys. Every large city has at least one store offering an amazing array of devices to inflict pain on immobilized victims. I looked in the phone book and found one right here in our area. It's called "Al's Cum Shop," which doesn't say much for the kinky community. Not only is *come* misspelled, it's not even grammatical. If it were "Come to Al's Shop," or something similar, it would make more sense. People should really give these things a little more thought.

Anyway, in addition to stores such as the unfortunately named example above, the Internet is crawling with websites selling BDSM equipment. A quick search revealed the following, just a few of many hundreds of applicable sites:

Crazy Bud's Discount Whips and Chains

Floggers "R" Us

Leather Betty's Whips and Used Postcards

Silent Night, Bloody Night, Tools of Torture

The Dark and Smelly Garden of Delights

Bad Vibrations

Wendell's House of Pointy Things

Mistress Juanita Dares You to Buy Something, You Creepy Little Turd

Führer Bob's House of Hurt

Wet and Sticky Toys

Admiral Gwen's Chamber of Pain and Stuff

The United States Internal Revenue Service

I'm not sure, but that last one may have been a mistake by the search engine. At any rate, I looked at these sites and found myself bewildered by many of the devices advertised. The purpose of a whip is certainly no puzzle but a lot of the other things kinky people like to play with are rather mysterious. Here is a list of some of the odder gizmos and their purpose:

Butterfly board: I kept running across these things on the bondage equipment websites. I can only assume there is some association between kinkiness and ichthyology; more specifically, in the collection and mounting of butterflies. When you think about it, that's an odd thing for a leather-clad dominant to be doing in a dank dungeon but then so many things are odd these days.

Sleepsack: This is a large leather or latex bag used to keep one's toys in while asleep. Why it's important to keep the toys in bed during rest isn't apparent but perhaps there is a problem in the kink community with things being stolen. The sleepsack I saw was covered with dozens of locking buckles so this may well be the case.

Interrogation chair: This isn't a toy, per se, but I wanted to include one piece of dungeon equipment here and I found this to be a particularly odd item. It's a heavy wooden chair just bursting with straps, restraints and other gadgets to keep a person immobile for long periods of time. Its primary use is for **scenes**, as kinksters like to call their encounters because they play out in much the same way a movie scene does. For example, one kinkster might say to another, "Hey, I had a great scene with Jen last night but I'm afraid the parrot will never be the same."

Likewise, the interrogation chair is often used in scenes where one person pretends to be a merciless captor who must get information from the "prisoner" by any means. During my ethnographic study of the kink community, I took part in such an interrogation scene, which took place in a small basement room with damp concrete walls, lit only by a bare light bulb hanging from the ceiling. My captor called herself Madame Payne. She was a tall woman, heavily made up and dressed in a black latex catsuit and thigh-high boots with impossibly tall heels. She spent almost an hour strapping me tightly into the interrogation chair, mumbling vague threats as she did so. This was the first time I had been bound in any way and my fear level increased as each buckle clicked shut.

Luckily, I was not gagged or blindfolded so I was able to mentally record what occurred as I listened to Madame Payne's heels click menacingly on the cracked cement floor as she circled me, a smile playing at her blood red lips.

"Who are you working for?" she snarled.

"At the moment, I'm a part-time clerk at Clayton's Books," I said. (I had recently taken a job there.)

She glanced at me and rolled her eyes. "You're not supposed to tell me what I want to know," she muttered, fondling a leather riding crop.

"I know, but it seems so terribly rude," I said.

Madame Payne stared at me. "I don't think you get it. If the scene's going to work, you have to resist."

I took a moment to mull this over, becoming increasingly aware of the many leather restraints sealing me to the chair. "That would seem to work against effective communication,"

I said in what I hoped was a respectful voice. "But I see we're only pretending here so I'll do my best."

She nodded. "Good. I'd hate to have to use *this* on you." She grabbed a flogger from an old wooden table and swished it over my head. "Now, who are you working for?"

A tingle of fear rose within me. My limbs ached for release as I struggled in vain against the chair. I felt myself getting pulled into the scene, thanks to this insidious confinement device. "I, uh, am employed at the Book Nook," I lied, gasping for breath.

Madame Payne rolled her eyes again. "Okay. The deal is, I ask the questions but you don't answer. You resist, and then I have to punish you. That's why you're here, right?"

I blushed and made my apologies.

"I have ways of making you talk." Madame Payne picked up a shiny metal device covered with spikes from a table and brandished it in my face. "Tell me—who sent you here?"

I tried to think but the menace of Madame Payne and my growing feeling of helplessness washed all sensible thought from my mind.

"Answer me!" she roared. "Who sent you here?"

"Well, no one really," I blurted in a shaky voice. "It was my own idea and—"

"Shit!" Madame Payne grimaced and slammed the spiky device on the table, creating a dent even a master carpenter couldn't repair. "How the hell am I supposed to do a scene when this idiot keeps talking?" she complained to someone standing behind me. "You deal with her. I give up. I'm going to beat the crap out of somebody."

As she clicked out of the room, I heard a man snicker but I couldn't move a muscle to see him. Finally, he stepped around the chair, treating me to a view of his tight leather costume covered in silver studs. He looked me in the eye, shaking his head. "What planet are you from?" he asked, fumbling to loosen the buckles holding me in place. "You might just be the worst submissive ever."

It took nearly as long to get out of the interrogation chair as it did to get in and I thought about the man's words while he unbuckled me. Of course, I was a bad submissive. I was, after all, posing as Mistress Dominique for the purposes of this book but I knew I'd have to work on at least pretending to be submissive in order to further my research.

"There you go, blondie," he said, finally freeing me from the interrogation chair. It was a relief to escape. My knees trembled from the intensity of the bondage and the scene in which I'd taken part. I had planned to engage in another scene that night but I felt so exhausted I went straight home and took a hot bath. The interrogation chair is definitely not for faint of heart.

Vampire glove: A particularly sinister-looking thing, it's basically a leather glove with a lot of nails or tacks sticking out of the palm and fingertips. What it has to do with vampires is unclear but perhaps if you put on a pair of these gloves and whack a victim upside their neck hard enough, they would start to bleed. What happens after that is too nasty to contemplate.

Van Buren sound: This is a particularly baffling thing. I've never actually seen a Van Buren sound nor is there a clear relationship between kinkiness and the eighth president of the United States, Martin Van Buren. It may be a sound reproduction device but there isn't any real way to know what kinds of sounds the former president made, since recording devices didn't exist during his lifetime. I suspect it's an apparatus that produces a replication of what people think Mr. Van Buren's voice sounded like. Perhaps it plays recordings of phrases such as, "I am the president. Bend over,

I want to spank you now," or "I've got a hot throbbing pocket veto, bitch." Personally, I think the Van Buren sound is terribly misnamed. Anyone who knows history would have chosen Herbert Hoover for such a device, as he was a known pervert, but Van Buren seems to be the overwhelming choice in the kink community.

Scene music: While we're on the subject of sound, a dungeon wouldn't be complete without music to help set the appropriate mood. I heard a lot of scene music played in dungeons during my research. It tended to be murky instrumental stuff featuring synthesizers played by Germans. But why not something bright and energetic? After all, lots of physical activity goes on in dungeons and you don't want to bring the participants down with music that has no life to it.

On a visit to a BDSM club in Sarasota, Florida, I decided to bring along a CD I thought would be helpful in establishing the proper mood. I politely waited until a particularly boring CD by a man named Death von Gruberstein or some such thing finished playing on the dungeon sound system then replaced it with my own selection. But when it began playing, people had fits! What's wrong with a nice, lively John Phillips Sousa march? I thought the dominants would have fun matching the strokes of their canes or floggers to the strong beat but it wasn't to be. All kinky activity came to a halt as everyone stared at the speakers, mouths hanging open like fish. Finally, a large dominant man dressed all in leather straps stomped over, pulled my CD from the player and smashed it to bits on the floor to the cheers of the assembled kinksters. It made me angry but the strap man held a large bullwhip in a meaty fist so I kept quiet.

Scrotal parachute: I wasn't able to discover who invented this device but it obviously wasn't anyone familiar with aerodynamics. We've all seen parachutes before—huge expanses of silk or nylon that do a fine job of catching the air and allowing the intrepid parachutist to glide gently to earth after they've leaped from an airplane.

The scrotal parachute is nothing like this, as I witnessed one evening when I infiltrated a leather bar in my guise as Mistress Dominique. At the height of the festivities, a submissive man staggered out on a balcony overlooking the bar. He pointed to his crotch, imprisoned in a scrotal parachute, which was nothing more than a small bit of leather with weights dangling from it. "I'm gonna fly!" he yelled in a slurred voice and then clumsily climbed over the railing and plummeted to the floor, some twenty feet below.

Let me say, at no time during his brief journey did the parachute exhibit even the slightest ability to break his fall or enable him to glide safely down. In fact, he dropped like a rock, landing face first on the concrete floor. Fortunately, someone called an ambulance to take him to the hospital, where he probably had a lot of explaining to do, if he ever recovered consciousness. Such a shame…

Violent wand: You know how sometimes after you walk across a carpet and then touch a doorknob you get a nasty shock? Well, that's basically what a violent wand does, except the shocks it administers are continuous. The wand consists of a plastic handle attached to an electrical source, with glass fittings in various shapes that attach to the wand's tip.

A dominant handed me a violent wand one night and gestured toward his sub, a woman who had been shackled to the wall. From what I understood, the wand is supposed to make a menacing buzzing sound while the dominant beats the crap out of the sub with it. So I flicked it on, my hand vibrating slightly as electricity flowed through the device, creating lovely purple sparks in the glass globe attached to the handle. It's not in my nature to hurt others but research is research, so I reared back and bashed the sub's back with the globe. Not surprisingly, the glass immediately broke into thousands of pieces, covering the sub's back with cuts. She also received a nasty jolt of electricity, which caused her to scream. In fact, she screamed so much that she began foaming at the mouth before suddenly losing consciousness.

I won't pretend to understand why anyone would want to be hit with a violent wand but after I struck the sub, all heck broke loose in the dungeon. A domme grabbed the wand, giving herself a terrible shock in the process, while others yelled incoherently at me. Perhaps that's the typical reaction when a wand is used properly but I'm not sure. At any rate, I sensed that the mood in the dungeon had turned ugly so I lost myself in the confusion and went home to watch *Masterpiece Theatre*.

Bondage tape: These days, the consumer can choose between many different types of tape: duct tape, masking tape, cellophane tape, electrical tape, ad infinitum. What the deuce might bondage tape be? As far as I can tell, it's a stretchy tape without much adhesive strength. If you can get a submissive to stand still long enough, it's possible to have an Egyptian mummification scene (as described in Chapter Two) by wrapping the sub from head to toe in this tape. However, I would definitely leave out the brain hook business. It may have been legal in ancient Egypt to remove people's brains but these days the authorities tend to frown on such things. I'm sure the submissive would be quite angry as well, although they probably wouldn't be capable of much emotion with their brains missing.

After the sub is securely wrapped in the bondage tape, the dominant usually steps back to admire their work. I suspect at that point the sub promptly topples over and whacks her head on a table or the floor but perhaps that's part of the fun. One never knows for sure.

Sadly, I only have enough space to describe a few examples of the vast supply of kinky toys available today. Indeed, an entire list of the standard kinky inventory would take up an entire book by itself! Those of you interested in further information are encouraged to consult your local yellow pages or conduct an Internet search for websites selling kinky toys. Those of you who are shocked and/or offended by the whole thing should try to stop thinking about it and not get so upset. I mean, no one is *making* you read this, right?

Chapter Four

Roleplaying—For when you just don't feel like yourself.

PLAYERS AND PLAYEES

As we noted earlier, kinky encounters are called **scenes** but the similarity to filmmaking terminology does not stop there. Kinky activities are often referred to as **play** and its participants as **players**. "We played in the dungeon last night and Millie's nipple fell off," someone might say, and other kinksters would know exactly what that person was talking about and nod approvingly.

Much of what constitutes kinky play involves the adoption of a persona, otherwise known as **roleplaying**. Chapter Two illustrated the process by which dominants adopt a title that explains their role, as in such monikers as Sir BadgerFiend or Ms. Itchy. Here we will examine some of the more popular roles and roleplaying activities. Note that many of these activities involve the use of costumes, props and even specially constructed sets, such as a dungeon or doctor's office.

AGE PLAY

From what I understand, this is a popular kink. At its most basic, it involves people taking on the characteristics of a particular age group that isn't their own. For example, some age players might enjoy regressing to babyhood, while others prefer to emulate people much older than themselves. Some people like to use this type of play to relieve the tensions that build up in the course of their daily lives or so I'm told.

Infantilism: This is the most popular form of age play. We all know people who like to act childish because they're big, stupid jerks. My cousin Pete comes to mind. Every Friday he gets drunk on cheap beer and like a moth attracted to a flame, shows up at my door. Last time, he drove his pickup truck through my front yard, making huge ruts and destroying my azaleas. The time before that, he vomited on my cat, PeeWee. Pete is the biggest jerk there is. Certainly, you can think of many people like this. Probably they should all be put into a huge rocket and shot off into space but that's awfully expensive, plus if they land on another planet and still act like jerks, that planet might get ticked off and launch an attack on Earth, leaving the planet a charred ball of rubble. That wouldn't be any good.

Aside from that, there are people who like to behave in a childish way as a sexual turn-on. People into infantilism find it pleasurable to regress to their childhood and be treated as babies. Most of these adult infants are men but women are known to participate in this kink as well.

Let's look at a typical series of events that form an erotic interaction between a middle-aged male infantilist and his wife, whom we will refer to as "Baby" and "Mommy" respectively, even though Baby is called Big Dave by his buddies at the country club. His wife is called Ted by her friends, for reasons that are unclear and should probably stay that way.

The scene begins with Baby and Mommy in their play space—the spare bedroom—which has been outfitted with a crib, a large supply of talcum power, a small chest of drawers for baby's diapers and other necessaries, and several cute pictures of duckies and bunnies. As she always does during kinky play, Mommy wears her "special sex outfit," a pirate costume complete with an eye patch. It's not clear why she does this. Baby would prefer that Mommy dress like a nurse or even a leather-clad dominatrix but Mommy likes dressing like a pirate. Perhaps her therapist knows why. Perhaps not. (For more information, see the discussion on **Piratism** below.)

The normal sequence of events for this scene goes as follows:

Mommy puts diaper on Baby.

Baby coos contentedly.

Mommy puts pacifier in Baby's mouth.

Baby smiles and gurgles.

Mommy goes the kitchen to make baby a bottle.

Baby cries.

Mommy returns and discovers that baby has made peepees.

Mommy changes diaper.

Baby is happy again.

Mommy goes back to kitchen and discovers that the formula has overheated and spilled all over the stove.

Baby cries.

Mommy checks diaper and finds that baby has made poopies.

Mommy changes diaper.

Baby makes cooing sounds.

Once again, Mommy returns to kitchen to clean up burnt formula from the stove.

Mommy breaks a nail while scraping the pan.

Baby cries.

Mommy discovers that baby has dropped his pacifier, which she replaces in baby's mouth.

Baby smiles and wiggles his tummy.

A little more slowly, Mommy heads back to the kitchen and tries to clean up the &(*$@!@! formula mess.

Baby cries.

Mommy checks diaper again and discovers baby has made more peepees. Where does it all come from? she wonders.

Mommy thinks for a moment, then takes baby to the nearest orphanage and dumps him on the front steps. Afterward, she cleans out the joint bank account and heads for Bermuda with Chuck, who lives next door and has a thing for women who dress as pirates.

Grumpies: Age play is not limited to those who wish to be babies. Some go in the opposite direction, pretending to be much older than they really are. Most of those who engage in this kink are men seeking an outlet for the frustration and anger that occur during the daily course of their lives. As a result, they don the persona of grumpy old men or **grumpies**, as they like to be known.

Interestingly, at least two motion pictures were made involving this particular kink. I think they were called *Grumpy Old Farts* and *Grumpy Old Farts Part 2*. If memory serves, Jack Lemmon starred in one or both films, a sad commentary on the decline of his career. If you wish to see these movies, they are likely available at shops that sell pornographic videos.

The grumpy experience usually begins with getting into character, so to speak, by dressing the part, a process that in itself becomes highly eroticized to its participants. Male grumpies usually don oversized white boxer shorts, a pair of dark slacks with a waistband reaching nearly to their nipples and a dress shirt buttoned all the way to the collar. They add to that a pair of black wingtip shoes (Florsheim is the preferred brand), white socks and black horn-rimmed glasses with frames far too large for their faces. The few women who practice this kink, known as grannies, adopt a costume consisting of a shapeless flowered housedress over a padded bra that is weighted to make their breasts appear to sag toward their knees. (Ick!) They finish the look with stockings rolled to just above the knee and sensible laced shoes with a short, thick heel.

Of course, both male and female grumpies wear gray wigs over their own hair. Males prefer wigs that make them appear to have thinning hair but some buy expensive skullcaps so as to appear bald. For grannies, the look is often gray hair pulled back into a tight bun, though some of the weirder grannies like the bald look as well.

For those grumpies into more extreme forms of play, adult diapers are a popular addition. If you have ever wandered by the adult diaper section of your local Kmart and seen a group of men huddled near the display, giggling and looking furtive, then you've spotted some grumpies.

Since this costume is not too outlandish, at least compared to a pink latex catsuit, it's easy for grumpies to act out their erotic scenes in public. In fact, making use of the reactions of innocent bystanders is an important component of satisfying their needs. This public behavior may be as simple as standing in the front yard screaming vague and often incoherent threats to the neighborhood children, such as "Stay out my yard, you little hooligans, or I'll do you to a turn!" or "You kids! Get out of my apple tree or I'll turn you inside out six days from November!"

Other grumpy play may be more confrontationally complex, as with those who wander into their local bookstore loudly demanding a copy of Lawrence Welk's biography and then causing a scene when they are told the store has none in stock. More adventuresome grumpies may even lightly whack the salesperson about the head and shoulders with their canes, becoming sexually aroused by the knowledge that it's unlikely anyone will retaliate against an old coot.

Equally important are the "toys" these kink practitioners use during their play. The most commonly used items are canes, hearing aids and umbrellas. In recent years, many age play fans have made use of the "Clapper," a device sold on late night television, in which a handclap turns an appliance on or off. One grumpy states that during lovemaking he plays an applause tape that causes his Clapper to turn his bedroom lights on and off hundreds of times per minute.

It wasn't easy, but I tracked down a grumpy for an interview. His given name is Trent but he prefers to be known as "Egbert" when in character. His favorite roleplay involves donning the typical grumpy outfit and performing errands that might seem routine to you and me but create intense arousal for him.

Trent/Egbert: *I got into the grumpy thing about five years ago. I was walking to the grocery store when I saw this old guy screaming bloody murder at his paperboy. Hell, I don't know why but I got hard as a rock. I couldn't get it out of my mind. The next day I took my girlfriend to a cafeteria and saw all these old people getting a senior discount and everything and that cinched it. I was hooked.*

That night I told my girlfriend I had some work to do at the office, but I really snuck out to a men's store that sells old guy clothes. I spent my whole paycheck that night on all kinds of elderly drag. I even bought a straw hat! The whole time I was scared stiff they might figure out what I was doing and kick me out of the store but nobody said anything. As soon as I got home I tore into the bags and tried on the clothes. Oh man! I never had a rush like that before! I masturbated until I passed out.

One thing led to another and pretty soon I maxed out my credit card buying more and more clothes, plus a lot of orthopedic dress shoes and a cane. I even got a pair of those huge black geeky glasses to wear, even though I don't need them. When I found a toupee with gray hair, the whole look was there. I was a grumpy and there was no turning back.

Eventually, I found some grump sites on the Internet and started hanging out in some chat rooms. The other grumpies were really supportive and gave me lots of great tips, like weird things to yell at people. The look on their faces gets me hot! They know I'm pissed off but they don't have a clue why I'm pissed or what I'm saying. I'll scream, "You little twerp! When I'm done with you, the Kaiser himself won't be able to put you back together!" They get nervous and back away in a hurry. I love it.

My girlfriend left me when she found out. I tried to keep it a secret but one night she walked in unexpectedly when I was dressed up. I got so scared, I whacked her a couple of times with my cane, just out of habit. She was seriously pissed when she found out it was me. I tried to get her to dress up like a granny but she looked at me like I was nuts and ran out of the house. I tried to call her a few times but she hung up on me. Later, the cops brought over a protection order, so that was that.

Sometimes I wish I'd never gotten into this. At first, it was okay to yell at kids and stuff but as time went on I got into more serious play. Last week I got seriously buzzed on Geritol and next thing I know, I'm standing in the front yard wearing nothing but my black socks and a truss, ranting about how the government is going to get rid of Medicare. Somebody called the cops and it took a lot of explaining to get out of that one. I can't quit, though. Nothing turns me on like this does. I don't know what I'm going to do.

Teenism: A psychiatrist acquaintance tells me the preferred medical term for this kink is *adolescentilism* but when I told a teeniest of this, he replied, "Yeah? Well, your shrink friend sucks. Or maybe he blows. Dumbass." Many conversations I had with teenists were similar in nature. I think I'm glad I don't have children.

Anyway, practitioners of teenism, primarily well-to-do middle-aged men and women, get a sexual high from dressing as surly teenagers and hanging out at local malls. Popular activities with teenists include staring sullenly at everyone who passes by, smoking cigarettes in front of the video arcade even though the entire mall is clearly marked as a "no smoking environment" and taunting the mall security guards.

Teenists have evolved a strict clothing code. For the girls, purple eye shadow, blood red lipstick and tight, revealing clothing are *de rigueur*. All the boys must wear a baseball cap and are further required to wear it backward. They must also be shod in a pair of expensive basketball shoes endorsed by an NBA player who has been arrested at least twice. Male teenists favor baggy jeans and wear them so low on their hips that their underwear sticks over the waistband quite prominently. This look appears to be an emulation of such popular rap musicians as DJ Iced Cold Tea and Master Funkwad. I'm not entirely sure about these names since I don't listen to rap music at all. As far as I'm concerned, most of it sounds like the hideous screams and moans of people caught in an exploding disco.

In recent years, both male and female teenists have adopted extensive facial piercings as part of their costume. I am assured that most of these piercings are temporary items, sold by websites and stores catering to this crowd. Temporary tattoos are also popular, though some hardcore teenists get permanent tattoos of their favorite rock band. Some of the more popular groups are, if I remember correctly, the Exploding Potato Conspiracy, George W. Bush's Left Toe, and Vomiting Giraffes Without a Clue. I miss the old days when groups had simple names like the Beatles and the Monkees.

I spent some time with a typical teenist in his usual habitat, the food court of a large mall in Paramus, New

Jersey. "Justin" is a white, forty-four year-old securities trader on Wall Street. He has been married twenty-one years and has three children. On the surface, he appears to live a typical middle class lifestyle. On many weekends, however, he can be found indulging in his favorite kink at the mall, where a large teeniest clique has formed. While sucking on an Orange Julius, he agreed to a brief interview. I should mention that at this time I was still struggling with my Mistress Dominique persona, particularly my look. On the day of the interview, I dressed mostly in denim, which I'll never do again. Strange, rough looking women kept staring at me and saying things like, "How are they hanging, butchy?" Anyway, here's the interview:

Mistress Dominique: You say you're a practitioner of teenism. In particular, you describe yourself as a *gansta*. What exactly do you do in pursuing your kink?

Justin: Yo, blood! What up? What up? Justin in da hizzhouse! I be hangin' with the road dogs at the mall. Hey, props to my peeps! Word!

MD: Excuse me?

Justin: You got to get jiggy wid it! It's a straight G, ho!

MD: I'm sorry, but I'm not following you at all.

Justin: I got to get me some stanky on my hangdown! Bag up some bitches! Word!

MD: What?

Justin: Ya got to get down with my bone! Booyah!

MD: Please stop that. It's very annoying.

Justin: Don't be dissing me, ho. Marinate, baby, marinate. Chill with the J-man, ya dig?

MD: Huh?

Justin: I wanna get busy wit' you. You look like a tasty thang.

MD: Are you trying to proposition me?

Justin: I gotta getta peep at yo' punami! I wanna turn you out, beeotch!

MD: You need a shovel put upside your head.

Justin: You ain't dope, sistah.

MD: Shut up.

CHARACTER PLAY

In addition to age play, many kinksters enjoy roleplay involving a special archetypal character. It isn't always clear why a particular characterization appeals to an individual. In fact, questions abound. Why would anyone derive sexual pleasure from dressing as a medieval knight or a cowboy? Knights spent much of their lives riding through the cold and rain before getting killed by a peasant armed with an axe. Cowboys slept outside all the time, ate nothing but beans and were covered with ticks, fleas and other vermin. That's fun?

It's obvious that the roots for these desires are buried deep in the individual's psyche, in those messy places where only psychiatrists and other qualified mental health workers dare to go. The following examples are but a taste of the myriad roles adopted by kinksters in their pursuit of sexual gratification. During the course of my research, I encountered people who got their kicks from emulating professional wrestlers, waitresses, the vice president of the United States, insurance agents and even a man who enjoys dressing as a plumber, complete with low slung pants that show off his butt cleavage to a disgusting degree. Well, if they are nothing else, kinky people are an endlessly creative bunch.

Piratism: Remember Mommy/Ted from the infantilism scenario above? As it turns out, she isn't the only one who gets off from dressing like a pirate. A quick Internet search turned up dozens of pirate groups—or *crews*, as they call themselves—located across the country. Further research uncovered an interesting pirate newsgroup, alt.sex.weird.pirates.ahoy. I joined this group under the name "EyePatchWench," which resulted in my obtaining the following interview with William T., known as Cap'n Stiffie by his friends in the pirate community.

Cap'n Stiffie: *Yeah, I don't know. Me and the wife like getting dressed up like pirates. I think she was the one who brought it up. Some friend of hers down the street dressed up like a pirate whenever she got it on with her husband. I think he liked to dress up as Babe Ruth—something like that. Anyways, when we do the pirate thing, my wife gets all hot and I get a boner like you wouldn't believe.*

It started out with us buying cheap pirate outfits and a couple of plastic swords one Halloween but lately we've been putting a lot of cash into it. Now we have real nice outfits and real swords. Last summer I built a 3/8-scale pirate ship in the backyard. Named her the Raging Maniac. *Cost a freakin' fortune, that thing did! The neighbors are pissed about it but I just told 'em I was a history buff.*

I like to board the Maniac *and pretend I'm a bloodthirsty sea captain. Thing is, my wife likes being a bloodthirsty sea captain too. It messes things up because neither of us gets to dominate the other, since we're both the same rank. We probably ought to work on that.*

We both wear hooks and eye patches and she just got a real stuffed parrot to wear on her shoulder. I'm kind of jealous about that. I tried putting one of them Beanie Baby parrots on my shoulder but it looked stupid and fell off all the time.

Our scenes start out when we scowl at each other a lot and say, "Arrrr, matey," and she makes her parrot say rude stuff like "Avast ye swabbie, is that a peg leg or are ye just glad to see me?" and we threaten to tie each other to the mizzenmast and flog each other. I guess it would be fun if one of us actually did tie the other one up and flog them but we never seem to do that. We just argue about who's more bloodthirsty and who has the best hook and stuff. Then we go back in the house and watch TV.

Other attempts to contact those who practice piratism met with little success. Apparently, these people are very private about their activities and my requests for further interviews met with either silence or threats to "split your head open with a marlin spike," whatever that is.

Authority figures: Many types of kinky play involve emulating people who serve in positions of authority. Schoolteachers are popular with people into this type of play, as are doctors, nurses, judges, police officers, corporate presidents and even politicians. Of course, if one is going to roleplay as an authority figure, one must have a partner who is willing to participate as the person over which they have control. The doctor must have a patient, the police officer must have a criminal and the office manager must have a subordinate.

Margo and Norm, a married couple, are very much into this type of play, particularly what they call the "evil head nurse" scenario. The most frequent and arousing scene they've developed involves Norm playing a man who has been injured in a car accident. He finds himself at the hospital emergency room, where Nurse Margo takes over his care and treatment:

Norm: Every time we do it, it's a little bit different. Most of the time, I'm hurt but not real seriously, just enough that Head Nurse Margo has to do things to get me better.

Margo: Being the nurse puts me in charge since Norm is injured and has to rely on me to relieve his suffering. The fun part is thinking up all kinds of evil things to do to him while he's at my mercy.

Norm: One time she decided I had a broken penis bone. I don't know if my penis has a bone in it but I guess they call it a "boner" for a reason.

Margo: It seemed like a good idea if he had a broken penis. That gave me an excuse to touch it a lot during my examination.

Norm: I really liked that part. It was the best scene we'd ever had, except for when I had to fill out the insurance papers.

Margo: My friend works at the local hospital so I had her get me the forms everyone has to fill out when they go to the ER. She brought me a huge stack of paperwork!

Norm: I don't get that. I had to sit on this really uncomfortable stool for over an hour filling in all these forms. When I finally got done, she took the papers and typed stuff into our computer for the longest time.

Margo: I had to enter all your information in the hospital databank, didn't I?

Norm: Yeah, I guess. After she finished typing, she said there was a problem with my ID number and she was going to have to call my insurance provider. She was on the phone over half an hour pretending to talk to the insurance company.

Margo: Our scenes have to be realistic or it isn't much fun.

Norm: I was sure glad to have that insurance business over with but then she sent me to the waiting room.

Margo: I made a waiting room in the kitchen. I lined up all our kitchen chairs in a row and put out some really old magazines I'd been saving up. It was cute!

Norm: But she made me sit in the kitchen for a couple of hours. The chairs got uncomfortable after a while and reading those old copies of *Vogue* and *Good Housekeeping* was boring.

Margo: We had to go by the book or it's not right. Anyway, it wasn't as long as he says and I got him in the treatment room soon enough.

Norm: That's when things got more interesting. At least for a while.

Margo: He needed treatment for a penile fracture and I had to put a cast on it. Norm was so surprised—I'd bought some casting material at the medical supply store.

Norm: I wish she hadn't.

Margo: I made a beautiful cast that completely covered his cock and balls. He couldn't touch them or even feel them. I felt like I was completely in control. It was wonderful.

Norm: Maybe for you. After a while I needed to take a whiz so bad I could taste it but my peehole was covered up!

Margo: I should have made him pee in a cup or something before we started. I just forgot. Oh well.

Norm: I don't want to talk about what happened when it came time to take off the cast.

Margo: The guy at the medical supply store said I'd need a big hammer to remove the cast. Looking back, I think he was kidding. How was I supposed to know?

Norm: I ended up a real emergency room. The nurses looked at us like we were crazy and laughed their heads off.

Margo: It was so unprofessional. I'd never laugh at a patient.

Norm: Next time we play, I'm going to have a cold or the flu. No one's going anywhere near my pecker!

Margo: Ooooh, that means you'll have to get a shot!

Norm: Oh, lord.

Royalty: For some kinksters, pedestrian authority figures aren't enough. These people go beyond what you might see in everyday life and become *regal*—kings, queens, lords, ladies, all manner of royalty. As noted in Chapter One, the Internet is full of people with titles such as Lord WhipGuy, Lady Laceration, Baron von Bruise, ad infinitum. For some, the title is enough but for others the desire to take on the trappings of royalty goes far beyond mere play.

Emily McLerhton is well known in kinky circles for her experiences dressing as royalty. That's her real name, by the way. She gave me a false name to use in this book but I misplaced it. My apologies, Emily. Anyway, upon her entry into the community, she was content to be known as Mistress Emily but after a while the idea of becoming a royal personage became too strong to resist. She bought a small parcel of land in rural southern Ohio, then took out large advertisements in newspapers throughout the area proclaiming her property as a new nation independent of the United States and that she was to be known henceforth as Emily, Queen of Bonerland. This caused a bit of a quandary, as people became confused as to whether Bonerland was the name of her country or a boast on Emily's part regarding her ability to cause men to have erections.

Emily's ad attracted dozens of submissive men to Bonerland (I'm assuming that was the name of her nation). Before long, she had a slave crew busily building her royal castle, complete with a moat stocked with hundreds of piranha fish obtained from a nearby pet store. (Emily also thought goldfish would be an attractive addition to the moat and bought several thousand for that purpose. They were instantly eaten by the piranhas.)

The slaves finished the castle after several months of intense labor. But since none of the men had any construction experience, the finished product looked mostly like a warehouse that had been hit by a tornado. Even so, Emily was pleased and moved in with her slaves, whom she kept in a constant state of nudity.

All went well in Bonerland as Queen Emily sat on her homemade plywood throne, issuing orders to her loyal subjects. Unfortunately, the happiness didn't last long. While Emily busily ruled her kingdom, an agent at the local FBI office in Columbus received an order he had placed for one of those singing fish. Remember those awful things? They were mounted on a plaque and twitched around while singing old Elvis tunes. Talk about torture! Lock someone in a small room with one of those evil devices. It won't take long before they agree to do anything you want.

Anyway, the fish arrived packed in old newspapers and in the process of removing his prize, the agent happened to see one of Emily's advertisements for Bonerland. Mistaking Emily's kinky empire for a dangerous religious cult, the agent rushed into the office of his supervisor, waving the crumpled newsprint wildly above his head. The supervisor took one look at the advertisement and jumped to the same conclusion as his subordinate. He ordered all six of his agents to launch a full-scale invasion of Bonerland.

The agents lacked a tank or any other kind of assault equipment, as the Columbus FBI office rarely had much to do. So, they rented a forklift, loaded it on a trailer and hauled it behind an old station wagon from the agency motor pool to the site of Emily's kingdom. Using a defective bullhorn that made his voice sound like that of an anguished squirrel, the agent in charge of the operation began yelling for the inhabitants of the castle to come out peaceably or risk an assault on their castle.

There was no response. After a great deal of discussion, the agent with the bullhorn gestured to the agent driving the forklift, who revved the engine a little to show they meant business.

Inside the castle, Queen Emily fumed. Her afternoon nap had been interrupted by the engine noise and the bullhorn, which she mistakenly thought was the sound of a pig being tortured. Because the slaves who built the castle forgot to include windows, they had no idea who was outside, so a representative was sent to open the drawbridge and have a look.

As the drawbridge lowered, the agent in charge grabbed the defective bullhorn and made an excited and unfortunately garbled announcement. Thinking he had been ordered to charge the castle, the agent driving the forklift roared ahead. He got about halfway across the badly constructed plywood drawbridge when it collapsed, plunging the agent and the forklift into the piranha-filled moat.

Hearing the agonized screams of the agent as the piranhas began nibbling his flesh, the other five agents sprang into action. They piled into the station wagon and roared at full speed toward what was left of the drawbridge, apparently in hopes of jumping the moat and landing inside the castle.

Meanwhile, Queen Emily listened to the report of the slave kneeling before her. Confused about the situation brewing outside, he told Emily that some teenagers had stolen a forklift and were attempting to enter the castle. Emily, who had been harassed at a mall by some **teenists** (see above), became irate and ordered her warrior slaves into action.

The slaves had meager weaponry: a few paintball guns loaded with red pellets, plus several electric flyswatters, gizmos that resemble a small tennis racket. Once charged with electrical current, they can be used to swat flying pests, frying them on impact. (It's not surprising that kinksters love the things, although I don't know if their use involves anyone dressing up like a bug before they are swatted.)

So armed, the slaves charged across the drawbridge as the FBI station wagon roared toward them. The agent driving the vehicle lost his nerve at the last second and attempted to steer away from the drawbridge, an ill-advised maneuver, which sent the vehicle into a violent roll. It careened down the bank of the moat, landing with a large splash that scared away the piranha and washed the forklift agent into the entrance of the castle. He was immediately greeted by the warrior slaves, some of whom whacked at him with the electric flyswatters while others fired their paintball guns.

The agents in the car, somewhat battered but not seriously hurt, scrambled out of the sinking vehicle and crawled up the outside edge of the moat. They turned to see their colleague, now covered in red paint, surrounded by naked slaves, who continued to beat the agent with the flyswatters. Mistaking the paint for blood, the agents drew their guns to fire, only to discover that their waterlogged weapons wouldn't function.

In frustration, one of the agents threw his gun at the slaves but it missed its intended target and bounced off the skull of the forklift agent, who lapsed into unconsciousness. At that point the warrior slaves stopped their hostilities and went back inside the castle, dragging the insensible agent with them before closing what little was left of the drawbridge.

The agent in charge managed to get his cell phone to work and made a frantic call to the regional FBI office in Cleveland. The supervisor who took the call listened as the highly agitated agent screamed about naked men, secret weapons, a forklift, piranhas and a castle. Shaking his head, the supervisor decided a deranged nut had somehow gotten his private number. He hung up on the agent and told his secretary to have his number changed.

Not knowing what else to do, the soaking wet agents abandoned the forklift, the station wagon and their fellow agent. They limped back to the Interstate, where they were given a lift by a group of Hare Krishnas traveling in an old school bus. During the ride, the agents decided not to file a report on their attempt to storm Queen Emily's castle and to deny that any such attempt had ever occurred.

When the manager of the rental company called the Columbus FBI office, wanting to know the whereabouts of his forklift, he was told it had been stolen by the agent they had left behind. The next day, a sheriff's deputy found the missing agent staggering down a dirt road, naked and covered with welts and dried red paint, babbling incoherently about Bonerland. He was arrested for stealing the forklift and remanded to the mental health wing of a local hospital, where he remains today.

Peace returned to Bonerland, but Queen Emily eventually grew bored with sitting on her uncomfortable plywood throne, especially when it became necessary each day for her to order a slave to remove the splinters lodged in her posterior. Finally, when the cold and snow of the Ohio winter made life miserable in the drafty and unheated castle, she snuck away late one night and took a position as a pastry chef at a popular local restaurant. There, she developed a food fetish that involved being covered in boysenberries and meringue. As far as anyone knows, the dozens of slaves she left behind still reside in the Bonerland castle, waiting for their Queen to return.

Clowns: Now really, what could be jollier than a clown? I love watching these colorful characters cavort at the circus. Who doesn't? More than a few people, as it turns out. They perceive clowns as sinister creatures to be feared and hated.

I'm told that Stephen King, a famous author, wrote a terrifying book about clowns called *They* or *Them* or *It*, something along those lines. I don't read much fiction, as research takes up most of my time, but I've been meaning to read one of those Harry Potter books, although they're probably out of print by now.

Anyway, clowns are one of the roles adopted by the kink community. Of course, kinky clowns (I want so much to write "kinky klowns" but my English professors would never forgive me.) aren't the type of character you'd want your children to see. These clowns aren't found in the circus but in shadowy dungeons, where they prey on their submissive victims.

I discovered a kinky clown one day while perusing the classified section of our local alternative newspaper. These ads make for highly interesting reading, by the way. Who knew there were so many bored housewives desperate for phone calls? They'd be better off getting out of the house and joining a gardening club or returning to school to pursue an advanced degree, as I did. At any rate, I spotted an ad for someone named Welty the Clown. The text of the ad was a giveaway as to Welty's kinky intentions:

Have you been naughty? Invite ***Welty the Clown*** *to your next adult party! I've got the equipment to turn a boring party into a WHORING party! Call now, losers! Let WELTY show you how to have a real good time! Cash only!*

I immediately phoned Welty, identifying myself as my alter ego, Mistress Dominique, and made arrangements to observe him at his next booking, which I took to be an all-male gathering of some sort. In order to attend, it was necessary that I pose as his assistant. I wasn't enthused about this but as I keep telling myself, research often takes us down challenging roads.

I met Welty on the appointed day at his trailer in the Beech Haven Mobile Home Park. Grinning, he ushered me inside. As I passed, he let out a ferocious belch and the small living room suddenly smelled of liquor. "Wait right there, baby," he slurred. "I got your outfit all ready to go."

He returned with a French maid's uniform, black with a ruffled white apron that tied in the back. I went into his filthy bathroom to put it on and discovered to my horror that the hem of the skirt barely covered my posterior. Even worse, the neckline plunged so low I feared the slightest movement would cause my breasts to easily escape the wispy black bra he provided. I decided to wear my own modest white underpants in place of the black silk thong Welty provided, though I did struggle into the black fishnet stockings and ridiculously tall heels. I finished by pinning a small ruffled hat on my honey blonde hair.

When I teetered out of the bathroom, I found Welty completing his own costume, a white latex clown suit covered in multicolored dots, with a wide black leather belt circling his expansive waist. With a shaky hand, he made up his face in the usual clown fashion, although much could be said for his talent in applying cosmetics. The finished job looked more like someone who had fallen face first into a painter's palette than anything else.

He finished by putting on a white skullcap with a thick fringe of brilliant red hair. I noticed with puzzlement that the skullcap had a spike protruding from the crown. Before I could ask its purpose, Welty picked up a quivering pink dildo and slid it over the spike so that it stood straight up. Every movement of his head made the dildo shake in a way that made me fairly queasy.

Grabbing a battered black doctor's bag, Welty led me to his car, an older model van with "Welty the Clown" spray painted on the side next to a menacing drawing of Welty himself. Looking back, I should have driven, as he seemed to have great difficulty with the relatively simple task of navigating the quiet neighborhood streets. We nearly struck several parked cars and barely missed running over a dog. When we arrived at our destination, Welty drove across the front yard rather than using the driveway, parking on a rosebush in full bloom. I shuddered to think what my friends at the Savvy Seeders garden club would think and breathed silent thanks they knew nothing of my research into kink.

Trying to keep my balance on the hideous heels, I followed Welty into the house and down to a basement rec room, where a dozen women had gathered in a circle of chairs.

"I thought this was a dude party," Welty slurred with a broad smile. "Looks like I got me a roomful of horny chicks!"

The women gawked at us in silence.

"How ya doing?" Welty roared, staggering to the nearest woman, who was dressed in a tasteful gray suit. Reaching in his bag, Welty removed a condom. "How about a balloon animal, wench?" he asked as the horrified woman shrunk back in her seat. Ignoring her reaction, Welty quickly inflated the condom and with a few deft moves shaped it into what appeared to be a breast, complete with a prominent nipple.

"Stick that under your bra, flattie!" Welty yelled, ignoring the woman's shrieks as he attempted to stuff the balloon down her blouse.

A tall woman stood, dressed in a navy pinstripe suit, her reddish-blonde hair perfectly sculpted. "I don't know who you are but if you don't leave immediately, I'll call the police!"

"Got me a feisty one," Welty growled. "I know what you want, you slutty bitch." He reached in the doctor's bag and pulled out a pair of silver handcuffs. Moving much faster than I thought he could, he lurched to the woman, who began screaming as he quickly put the handcuffs on her.

More pandemonium followed as the remaining women scuttled from their chairs and huddled in a corner. Up to this point, I had stood near Welty, watching events unfold as if in a dream. I was startled out of my reverie when an older woman in a lime green pantsuit turned pleading eyes toward me. "Please, there must be some good in you," she wailed. "Repent now, before it's too late. Reject your sinful ways and help us."

I suddenly became very conscious of my revealing costume. All I wanted to do was flee but Welty had other ideas. He grabbed my arm and led me to the huddled women, the pink dildo on his head bobbing obscenely.

"This is my whore!" he shouted, shoving me toward the women, who let out a horrified gasp. Just as I feared, the bra had failed in its containment duties, and my left breast had popped out of the plunging neckline of my dress.

Welty giggled and withdrew a fierce leather flogger from his bag. "Who's my pain slut?" he howled. "Who wants to feel the sweet ecstasy of torture?" He flicked the flogger at a tiny woman in a floral print dress. "You look like the type, bitch. Welty wants a piece of ass! Give it up, babe!"

The woman fainted dead away, banging her head on a folding chair as she slid to the floor. I clenched and unclenched my hands, completely at a loss. Is this how a clown scene was supposed to go? It felt wrong, somehow, horribly wrong.

A stout woman in a brown pantsuit pointed at me. "Stop your whoring ways now!" she yelled in a husky voice. "Make this heathen leave us in peace!"

The woman's brave words had a galvanizing effect on the others. As Welty pulled a length of chain from his bag, they attacked.

"What the hell?" he screamed as they fell on him, scratching, kicking and biting. One woman gave the clown a particularly hard whack in the face with a large Bible. It was then I noticed that most of them had Bibles and were putting them to good use as weapons.

"You stupid bitches!" Welty yelled as the brown pantsuit woman leveled a vicious kick at the dildo on his head. "This shit costs money!" The room filled with angry, high-pitched shrieks as the women battered Welty even harder.

I found myself clambering up the stairs as fast as my heels would allow. When I burst from the basement door into the kitchen, I nearly ran down an elderly woman holding a china platter piled with brownies. There was a moment of silence then she dropped the platter. It exploded into pieces, sending brownies skittering everywhere.

Grabbing a whisk from the sink, she glared my exposed breast with blazing eyes. "Whore of Babylon! Strumpet! Harlot! How dare you bring evil into this house!"

She whacked me a good one on the head with the whisk. In my attempt to evade the blow, I broke a heel. Quickly shedding the awful shoes, I ran for the back door, but not before the woman whacked me several more times. I had no idea a whisk could be such an efficient weapon.

The lights from an approaching police car painted the darkness red and blue as I ran through the backyard and managed to scale a fence into an alley. I turned for a moment and listened to the crashes and muffled screams from the basement. Then I ran for all I was worth, blistering my bare feet something awful on the long trip back to Welty's trailer. Luckily, he left the door unlocked and I quickly changed clothes, got into my car and skedaddled for home, holding my breath every time I saw a police cruiser.

The next morning I picked up the newspaper with great trepidation. Sure enough, our misadventure from the night before had made the front page. It turned out Welty had entered the wrong house and invaded a meeting of the Baptist Women's Bible Study group of Lindale Heights.

According to the story, the women had beaten Welty severely and had to be restrained by the police from inflicting even more damage on the man. The mug shot next to the story showed their handiwork. Welty's latex costume hung in tatters and both of his eyes were blackened and swollen. A trickle of blood ran from his nose and his lips were badly cut.

Next to the picture was an artist's rendition of a woman, and I realized with a thrill of horror it was meant to be me. Fortunately, the Baptist women were so distraught that they described me badly—in fact, the drawing looked more like a stringy-haired witch from a fairy tale than yours truly. If I hadn't been so relieved, I would have been insulted. After all, I have a smallish nose, not a long thin one covered with warts, and I don't have sunken cheeks or bulging, bloodshot eyes.

I allowed myself to relax when I finished the article and saw that I hadn't been identified by name, although Welty's attorney was quoted as saying the events of the previous night were the fault of an "experienced prostitute who led my client down a terrible, sordid path."

It was then I realized that being a good ethnographer requires great courage. I debated with myself for some time, wondering if I had the fortitude to continue my research. But then I thought about Uncle Henry and I felt his spirit with me, guiding me, granting me the fortitude to continue along the rocky road of kink. And so I did.

Chapter Five

Fetishes—Why that rubber glove is just so darned fun!

ꟙ

WHAT IS IT?

One of Uncle Henry's books defined **fetish** as a strong sexual attachment to an item, usually an article of clothing, a body part or sensory experience. Actually, the definition went into more detail than that but I forgot which book I was reading at the time. The gist of it is that while a particular item may mean nothing to you or me, if you wave that item at a person who has a fetish for it, they'll get all hot and bothered even though they have no idea why.

It must be awful to have a fetish. What if you had a fetish for white tube socks? You could never go to a health club because you'd be squirming around getting all excited and not paying attention to where you were going and get entangled in one of those weight-training gizmos. Or, what if you saw an elderly woman wandering down the street wearing tube socks? You'd start fantasizing about taking her home for some hot action and accidentally walk in front of a bus. This fetish thing seems fraught with peril.

There's also the matter of practicality. What if someone had a fetish for large buildings? You can't exactly collect them, and you certainly can't fondle a building in the privacy of your own bedroom. I don't know anyone like that but if I did, I'd feel sorry for them. I can imagine them lurking downtown, grabbing a surreptitious feel of the brickwork in order to get their *jollies*, as the kids say these days.

Fetishes are quite common and you never know who might harbor one. My cousin Edna, who lives in Minnesota, complained on the phone the other day about her husband, Chester. She said Chester was obsessed with buying bad cars, spending all his time in the garage, trying in vain to get them running properly.

The way she described his affliction got my attention. Could Chester have a fetish for malfunctioning cars? Hopefully not. I'd hate to think of him buying clunkers like Yugos or Pacers just to experience a sexual thrill. Those Renault Alliances weren't very good cars, either. I had one once. It never ran right and rusted out almost immediately. Perhaps Chester would get excited about it, although the mental image of him rubbing the fenders and drooling over the rust spots is unpleasant, to say the least.

Let's leave Cousin Chester and examine some of the more common fetishes found in the kink community.

Latex: One of the most popular fetishes involves latex clothing. My experiences indicate that there are many people who get incredibly turned on by wearing rubber clothing—bras, hosiery, hoods, dresses, gloves, you name it. For some, the fetish concerns just one particular item; for others, any clothing made of latex is fine and dandy. I sometimes wonder if my doctor isn't one of the former group. Every time I see him, the first thing he does is snap on a pair of latex gloves. It's insulting, really. I consider myself a very clean person and I don't think the gloves are necessary. Perhaps I should find a doctor who isn't so kinky.

Personally, I don't understand why latex is such a big deal. I like to keep a clean house, which means I frequently put on rubber gloves in order to do the dishes or clean the bathtub. So what? There's nothing erotic about scrubbing a nasty ring of scum from the tub. Or is there? I suspect someone will write to tell me filthy bathtubs excite them but that's a bit of information I could do without.

I was able to locate one couple who like to play with latex, or at least they used to. They didn't want to reveal their real names, so we'll call them Chuck and Tammy. As always, I conducted the interview in my guise as Mistress Dominique. I wanted to fit in with the fetish crowd for this interview, so I wore a yellow PVC raincoat I found at a garage sale, a pair of black rubber hip waders Uncle Henry left behind—he was an avid fisherman—and my aforementioned tub cleaning gloves. I don't know where I went wrong, but my outfit seemed to provoke much amusement from nearly everyone I encountered, even the fetishists.

Mistress Dominique: Tell me how you got started with latex.

Chuck: I found some magazines with pictures of people dressed in latex outfits.

Tammy: Oh, you found them, did you? Huh.

Chuck: Yes, I found them. At work. Somebody must have brought them to work and left them by mistake.

Tammy: You're a dentist! Who would bring pornographic magazines to a dentist's office? Linda, the slutty hygienist?

Chuck: She's not a slut, Lisa. You just don't like her.

Tammy: Whatever. You keep your hands off of her. And don't use my real name! I'm supposed to be Tammy.

Chuck: Like I was saying, I saw these pictures of people dressed in latex and it intrigued me. I started thinking it would be fun to try with Li—I mean, Tammy.

Tammy: When he showed me the pictures I thought it was weird but our sex life had gone sour, so I figured it wouldn't hurt to try it.

Chuck: Oh, it was sour, was it? Thanks a lot. Maybe giving Linda a hop in the sack wouldn't be such a bad idea after all.

Tammy: You just try it, Tom Robesson and see what happens!

Chuck: Shut up! I'm Chuck, remember?

MD: Could we get back to the latex thing?

Chuck: Oh yeah. Sorry. So, one day Lisa—

Tammy: I'm Tammy, dammit!

Chuck: Sorry. So one day Tammy decides to tie me up. I didn't know what was going on but she said I was her helpless latex slave, so I let her do it. It turned me on.

Tammy: I have to admit, I liked seeing him helpless on the bed. After I got him tied down, I went out to the garage for my big surprise.

Chuck: Some surprise.

Tammy: Hey, you said you wanted to try the latex thing!

Chuck: It wasn't as much fun as it looked in the magazine.

Tammy: You got what you asked for, so no complaining.

Chuck: I guess so. Thanks a heap.

MD: Excuse me, but what was the big surprise?

Tammy: Well, after he went on and on about the latex thing, I was watching TV and saw a commercial with that Bob Vila guy who Tom thinks is so great. I started to mute the TV so I wouldn't have to hear him go on about tools but then he started talking about latex paint. That gave me an idea, so the next day I went to Sears and bought a gallon of latex house paint.

Chuck: It was black paint. They had to make it up special.

Tammy: So, after I got Tom—

Chuck: I'm Chuck!

Tammy: Okay, okay. After I got Chuck tied down, I brought in the paint and started covering him with it. It made a horrible mess. I was glad I put down a tarp first.

Chuck: I hated it! The paint smelled awful and the roller she used tickled a lot. When she started painting my face it got up my nose and in my mouth. I thought I was going to choke to death.

Tammy: I tried to make him look like the people in the pictures but I must have done something wrong. He just looked like a big old lumpy blob of black paint.

Chuck: It was terrible. It made a huge mess of the bedroom and I spent two hours in the shower trying to get the paint off. It never did come out of my hair. Everyone at the office thinks I dyed my hair black to look younger or something. Linda keeps coming on to me.

Tammy: If she tries it again she'll be cleaning teeth with stumps for hands, you hear me, Tom?

Chuck: Yeah. I hear.

Tammy: And no more of that stupid kinky stuff.

Chuck: All right, already! Give it a rest!

Furries: While perusing the Internet, I stumbled upon a group of people who call themselves *furries*. They seem to have a fetish for dressing up as such anthropomorphic animals as Mickey Mouse, Huckleberry Hound, Bullwinkle J. Moose and the Teenage Mutant Ninja Turtles. Technically speaking, turtles don't have fur. Perhaps there's a subset group called shellies or slimies, something of the sort.

These people also love to dress up as Japanese *anime* characters. I don't watch much anime, though I do see it from time to time when I accidentally press the wrong button on the TV remote. Furries are attracted to anime because the shows are full of people who are half-cat or half-spaniel, that sort of thing. Personally, I find anime boring. It consists mostly of a character screaming, "I am more powerful than you!" and another character screaming back, "No! I am more powerful than you!" This argument goes on for quite a while and then they fight for the remainder of the program. Give me a good Agatha Christie movie any day.

Anyway, the main point is that furries have a fetish for dressing in animal outfits and become highly aroused simply at the thought of wearing their furry suits. And once they are dressed, they adopt a furry persona to match their new appearance, a persona so powerful that its use dictates the wearer's sexual behavior. In fact, some furries become so lost in their fetish they can only achieve sexual fulfillment while wearing their badger suit or whatever animal turns them on.

"Mike" is a furry, though his fetish involves feathers rather than fur. His interest in furry activities began innocently enough but as we will see, he is in an advanced state of fetishistic behavior.

Mike: *Yeah, I have a fetish. I know some guys have fetishes for high-heeled shoes or cheerleader panties, but I think my fetish is a lot more interesting than that stuff.*

I'm into owls. They're so damned sexy! I don't know why, but when I think about owls I get a stiffie like you wouldn't believe. It didn't take much at first. I got a few owl pictures I'd look at while masturbating and then I found some stuffed owls I keep in the bedroom. I think there's eighty or ninety in there right now. Then one day I found some owl sheets in a catalog. Oh man! I made my wife put them on the bed every time we had sex. And then I got a CD of owl sounds to play while we did it. I loved it!

The tough thing about a fetish is that you always want more and more of it. My wife got ticked off about the whole thing because she didn't understand why owls are so sexy. She tried, sometimes. Once I got her to yell "Hoot! Hoot!" when I came. That was great, so I told her I'd yell "Hoot! Hoot!" when she came but she said she had a headache and wanted to go to sleep and would I please turn off the stupid owl CD. That was a letdown.

One day I heard they opened a Hooters over in Altamont. Oh man! A whole restaurant about owls! I hustled Becky into the car and we got over there in a big hurry. When I walked in the door I was so hot I thought I'd explode but I have to admit, the place was a letdown. They didn't have that many owls around, mostly the Hooters logo on those tight t-shirts they make the waitresses wear. Big deal. Plus, the chicken strips I ordered weren't that great and Becky wasn't too thrilled with her Hooterburger. She glared at me the whole time and kept saying what an idiot I was to drive three hundred miles just to eat a hamburger. I don't think she talked to me once all the way home.

After that, I kept the owl thing quiet for a while but then I thought maybe she'd get into it more if I added some really sexy owl stuff. So I cashed in some bonds and did it up right. I spent hours getting my surprise ready then I called her into the bedroom. I was dressed up in the most incredible owl costume, with real owl feathers. Cost a fortune, but it had the sexiest beak I've ever seen. Who could look at that and not get hot? And it gets even better. I threw a bunch of pinecones and bark on the bed and the floor and I had the owl CD going full blast. I was going to have some dead mice around because that's what owls eat but I couldn't find any.

Well, I figured she'd come just from seeing what I'd done but all she did was stare. Her mouth moved some but no words came out. Then I pointed to my crotch and asked her to check the really special surprise I had for her. She shook her head and started trembling so I did it for her. I pulled down my zipper and there was my dick all dressed up in a little owl suit of its own! I said, "Look, it's Little Hootie, he wants to touch you!" Becky screamed and ran out of the house. I haven't seen her since. I hope she's okay.

Uniforms: Many people have a fetish for uniforms but not necessarily those of a bizarre nature, like those worn by the pirate couple in the previous chapter. Quite the contrary, the uniform fetishist often prefers outfits you might see in everyday life, such as those worn by nurses, police officers or maids.

John has a fetish for Kmart uniforms, particularly those smocks Kmart makes their employees wear. You can't miss them, as they're a particularly icky pale green, a color that not only doesn't appear anywhere in nature but shouldn't appear anywhere in the home of a person with good taste. Come to think of it, where was Martha Stewart when this decision was made? Surely a woman of her taste would have done something. Perhaps there are hidden sinister forces at work. I shall keep my eyes open next time I shop at Kmart.

But back to John. He gets excited when his wife, Verna, puts on one of those horrid smocks. You know, the more I think about it, the more I'm convinced something awful is afoot at Kmart. I don't know whom the shadowy people behind this smock thing might be but they must be stopped. I will write my congressman about this and I suggest you do the same.

Now, as I was saying, John gets all excited about the ugly smocks and engages in whatever fantasy scene he and Verna have scripted for the evening's fun. John was nice enough to describe one such scene:

John: *Verna is the best. Last week she called me at work and talked in a real low, sexy voice. She told me not to be late getting home because there was going to be a "big sale at the store". Hell, I knew what that meant. I didn't get a lick of work done the rest of the afternoon, just thinking about it.*

When I got home she was wearing that Kmart smock of hers and looking real good. Then she started talking into an empty baked bean can so her voice sounded all tinny, like through a loudspeaker. She says, "The time is now 9:45. Your Kmart store closes in fifteen minutes. Finish your shopping now, you big bad boy, or I'll have to take you back to the stockroom for hot throbbing sex!" Oh yeah! Soon as I heard that, the cobra was ready to climb out of my pants and strike!

Another time we were playing and I pretended to shop for a new set of wiper blades for the Buick. Suddenly I hear her voice again, like she was on the loudspeaker: "Attention Kmart shoppers. We are running a blue light special in aisle five. You know, aisle five, where the lingerie is. The sexy lingerie. Don't bother coming to aisle five unless you're a big, strong, manly sort of man."

I knew what I was supposed to do. I pretended to go over to aisle five, which is actually the hallway leading into the kitchen, and there was Verna, dressed in her smock, and black stockings, and real sexy heels. I almost got off just from looking at her. That was amazing!

Smell: While most fetishes are centered on particular objects, some fetishists react to more intangible stimuli, such as aromas. Many rubber lovers, for example, say the smell of latex clothing is even more intoxicating than the rubber garments they love to wear. Likewise, many adult babies get quite excited about the smell of baby powder. I once talked to a man who claimed to have a fetish for the smell and feel of powdered bathroom cleanser. Oh, he went on and on about it, until I finally let him come over and clean the downstairs bath. What a mistake that was! He did a horrible job on the tub and while he was cleaning the toilet, he was overcome by the fumes and passed out. It's a good thing I heard his head splash into the toilet water or he would have drowned for sure.

I learned a great deal about aroma fetishists when I received an email touting a mailing list catering to people with a fetish for smelly shoes, socks and underwear. At first, I thought it was a sick joke but I discovered to my amazement that it's not only real, but also very popular. In order to give you an idea of what this fetish entails, I reproduce below a sample of the messages I saw one evening on that email list, *Ruth's Smell of Love*:

Message: Finding vids

05-September-03: 05:48:18

I heard somebody's got some vdeos [sic] of women's feet after they walked through cow patties. Where can I get these??!!!!!

Marco69

Message: Dr. Scholl

05-September-03: 05:53:02

Anybody got any used Dr. Scholl's sandals worn by a female?? How about a vidoe [sic] of a female hitting a man with Dr. Scholl's sandals? Also, what about a female masturbating with a Dr. Scholl's sandal? What about a female throwing a Dr. Scholl's sandal at a dog?

I'm a Scholl Man!

Message: Panties and stuff

05-September-03: 05:54:42

I am a struggling female college student and barely legal. I have panties, nylons, sweat socks, shorts and other stuff for sale if you want to smell my stuff. It's pretty smelly stuff because it's been sitting around a while.

For more info, send $5.00 to:

Pattie's Stuff

P.O. Box 674
Linghampton, RI 07242

Message: HER FEET STINK!

05-September-03: 05:55:19

MY WIFE’S SHOES STINK LIKE NOBODY’S BUSINESS! I’M NOT TALKING ABOUT YOUR USUAL STINK—THIS IS UNBELIEVABLE. IT WOULD KILL MOST PEOPLE TO SMELL HER SHOES BUT IF YOU LIKE TO LIVE DANGEROUSLY, I WILL SEND YOU A PAIR OF SHOES SHE’S WORN FOR AWHILE. I’M TELLING YOU, THESE THINGS WILL PEEL YOUR WALLPAPER OFF. I’M SELLING THEM CHEAP JUST TO GET THEM OUT OF THE HOUSE!

WRITE ME AT BOX 7564L, BAJOREK, NEW JERSEY, 10122 FOR MORE INFO AND PRICE LIST. HELP ME OUT! I’M NOT KIDDING!!!

WILLIE

Message: NURSE’S SOCKS!!!

05-September-03: 05:57:42

I am a struggling nursing student. BUY MY SWEATY NURSING SOCKS NOW!!!!

GO TO www.nursesocks.com

nUrSe NaNcY

Message: SOCKS!!!!!

05-September-03: 06:12:33

I’m a sexy struggling nurse and my feet really get sweaty and stinky after walking around the hospital all day. Why don’t you buy my YUMMY worn socks? You know you want to! Yesterday, some old guy threw up on my shoes and some of it got on my socks. Will you be the lucky one who gets that pair??? Email me, HOT NURSE, at: strugglinghotnurses@nursemail.com

YOU KNOW YOU WANT TO!

HOT NURSE

Message: Re: HER FEET STINK!

05-September-03: 06:41:29

Willie wrote:

>>MY WIFE'S SHOES STINK LIKE NOBODY'S BUSINESS! I'M NOT TALKING ABOUT YOUR USUAL STINK—THIS IS UNBELIEVABLE. IT WOULD KILL MOST PEOPLE TO SMELL HER SHOES BUT IF YOU LIKE TO >>LIVE DANGEROUSLY, I WILL SEND YOU A PAIR OF SHOES SHE'S WORN FOR AWHILE. I'M TELLING YOU, THESE THINGS WILL PEEL YOUR >>FREAKIN WALLPAPER. I'M SELLING THEM CHEAP JUST TO GET THEM OUT OF THE HOUSE!

Mitch wrote back:

What about her underwear? Do they stink too? I like to wear women's panties and shoes and I like it when they're really smelly. I mean, REALLY really smelly, to the point where you could pass out or even die from it.

Also, I like to wear women's pants, leggings, hose, leotards, stockings, tights, socks and hats. Sned [sic] me a price list for all that stuff. Make sure it really stinks, though.

Mitch69

Message: Teacher's SOCKS

05-September-03: 07:01:01

I am a struggling school teacher and the only way I can afford to buy new shoes is to sell my old shoes. If you want to have my old shoes you can buy them at my website, www.missmarysshoes.com. I have a really old pair I just put up for sale. I think my Odor Eaters stopped working because they really reek. One of my students noticed and said, "Man, what died in here!" and another student vomited all over himself so you know this particular pair is really ripe.

Miss Mary

Message: Secretary panties

05-September-03: 07:30:31

Hello, I am a 25-year old struggling secretary. I have made a website to make some extra cash. I have been saving up all my panties from this summer, when I really got wet and sweaty. I have to constantly pull my panties out of my asscrack [sic] so they get real stinky and, of course, they have skidmarks. Sometimes I don't make it to the bathroom when I have to pee so that makes another kind of mess. Sometimes I get horney [sic] and masturbate with them too. The whole pile of panties has been sitting in the back of the closet for a long time and it's getting so stinky I have a hard time keeping the dogs out of there, plus some bugs got in the closet and started living in my panties. That's how smelly they are. If you want to buy my panties go to my site at www.secretarypanties.com. I accept Visa, Mastercard, Diner's Club, American Express, Carte Blanche and Discover. Hurry up and buy them before more of those bugs get on them.

Helen T.

Message: BE A MAN!!!!!!

05-September-03: 07:54:44

Why waste your time with sock [sic] or shoes? Get the real thing! At Molly's Garden we have a huge selection of used pads, tampons and panties. Guaranteed to give you a massive boner! All of our products are from struggling secretaries and nurses so you know we aren't ripping you off!

Molly's Garden: www.mollysgarden.org

Message: Re: Dr. Scholl

05-September-03: 08:50:34

Henry wrote:

>>Anybody got any used Dr. Scholl's sandals that have been worn by a female?? How about a vidoe of a female hitting a man with Dr. Scholl's sandals? Also, what about a female masturbating with a Dr. Scholl's sandal? What about a female throwing a Dr. Scholl's sandal at a dog?

sandal man's reply:

I have a video of Mistress Jenna from Vegas slapping around a guy who looks like Mr. [sic] Scholl. He's a really old guy so after a few good hits he gets pretty wobbly and falls down but they keep hitting him anyway. [T]hey knocked the shit out that old guy. Write me if you want to know more.

sandal man

Message: BUY THE BEST!!!!!!

05-September-03: 09:11:08

I am a struggling waitress. They don't pay us shit so I have to earn extra money by selling my panties. MINE ARE THE BEST!!!!! Others put their panties in an envelope and by the time it gets to you it smells like the post office. I sell only WET STAINED PANTIES that I seal in a zip lock bag fresh for your enjoyment. Sometimes I even put in some toenail clippings if I've just trimmed my nails. DON'T SETTLE FOR SECOND BEST!!! Write me today at pantyodorgirl@webcast.com

stefanie69

Well, you get the idea. The olfactory sense is a powerful one and drives some kinksters to do strange things. It's a shame all those struggling waitresses, teachers and nurses have to resort to selling their shoes and undergarments. If they were paid a fair wage, none of this would be necessary.

Food: I wasn't surprised to discover many people have a fetish for particular kinds of food. Now that I've learned something about fetishes, I wonder about my cousin Sue, who has a thing for bratwurst. I like a good bratwurst as much as the next person but Sue goes far beyond that. Once we went to an Oktoberfest celebration and the first thing she did was run to a bratwurst stand. She bought a plain one and heaved the bun away as though it was poison. Unfortunately, the bun whacked an elderly gentleman in the back of the head. He must have been German because he turned and screamed at us in what sounded like German. Then he started waving his arms and howling about Poland—at least I think it was Poland—and then he went on about the Sudetenland, whatever that is. Finally, another elderly gentleman took him by the shoulder and led him away. We could still hear him shouting ten minutes later. Such a temper! Anyway, Sue stands there clutching the bratwurst, grinning like a madwoman and running her fingers up and down the length of the thing. For a moment, I thought she was worried the meat was contaminated but before I could say anything, she slid the whole thing in her mouth and pulled it out again, over and over.

This attracted a fair amount of unwanted attention, mostly from men. It got worse when Sue began moaning and swaying back and forth. I don't know what went through her head but I was terrifically relieved when she let out one last moan and finally ate the darned thing. When she finished, smiling manically with grease dribbling down her chin, the group of men surrounding us broke into applause. They wouldn't leave us alone after that, following us everywhere. Needless to say, that was the last time I went with Sue to Oktoberfest or any festival where bratwurst can be found.

Perhaps Sue is into **sploshing**, the name food fetishists give to their favorite activity, which involves immersing oneself and others in various foodstuffs. From what I've been able to discover, most any food can be utilized in sploshing, but the general preference is for foods that are sticky and/or slimy. Think of it as a sexy food fight.

I was fortunate enough to attend a splosh, thanks to a veteran food fetishist I met at a meeting of the local BDSM group, who call themselves The Velvet Fist in the Iron Glove or some such thing. I didn't like attending their functions—called **munches** by kinky folk—because the men always assumed I was submissive and wanted to beat me with whatever implement lie at hand. When I told them I was Mistress Dominique they'd laugh and poke each other in the ribs. Who needs that?

My food fetish acquaintance, known as "Sauce Boy," agreed to introduce me to his friends so that I could take part in a sploshing scene. Sauce Boy, as befits his moniker, is known among his fellow sploshers for his love of sauces, particularly tomato sauce. He related to me a particularly heartbreaking tale in which he dumped a 128-ounce can of spaghetti sauce on a woman with a severe allergy to the stuff. She promptly swelled up like a balloon and had to be treated at a nearby emergency room, so it was a long time before Sauce Boy was welcomed back to the group. He now specializes in white wine sauces and occasionally, tartar sauce.

My introduction to sploshing began on a cool fall evening, when I met Sauce Boy in front of an attractive Tudor house in the suburbs, not at all what I expected. Actually, I'm not sure what I expected. Perhaps a ramshackle house with rotting piles of garbage heaped everywhere. This was certainly not the case as I entered the home and found myself in a living room decorated in Danish Modern, the walls covered with Impressionist paintings. Sauce Boy introduced me to the host for the evening's festivities, a tall, handsome man who called himself "Chef Boy-O-Boy".

At first, it appeared to be a run-of-the-mill party. I spent a pleasant hour mingling with the other dozen guests as we sat in the spacious living room, chatting amiably while sipping wine and margaritas. My cohorts looked to be well-dressed, highly educated and probably engaged in white-collar pursuits. Again, not what I expected.

The casual atmosphere suddenly turned tense when Chef Boy-O-Boy smiled and asked everyone to leave the room. As we were herded into the dining area, our host unrolled a large plastic tarp and with practiced ease quickly covered the carpeting and furniture in the living room.

Responding to an unspoken cue, the other guests began removing their clothing. As I watched a short, chunky gentleman remove his pinstriped suit and fold it neatly away on the dining room table, I had a sudden fear that Sauce Boy had inadvertently brought me to an orgy. Noticing my stare, the chunky man turned and looked at me expectantly but I hadn't planned on disrobing, as I prefer to remain clothed unless I'm in the bath.

When the group finished taking off their clothes, they reached into the bookbags they had brought and removed cans and jars of food. By the way, most of the bookbags were emblazoned with the NPR logo. I've tried to figure out if that is significant but so far the answer has eluded me. Now, when I listen to NPR, I can't help but wonder what's going on in the studio we can't see. Perhaps they deliver the news while covered in warm tapioca. Who knows?

The sploshing began when a young woman opened a large can of chocolate syrup and dumped it over her own head. As the crowd broke out in applause, she threw herself on the tarp and began rolling in the chocolate. The excitement in the room rose palpably as the others joined in, throwing honey, soup, mayonnaise, pudding and other gooey foods on the floor and then jumping in it, shouting and laughing.

Despite my pledge to uphold ethnological protocol, which meant becoming a participant in the sploshing, I felt my courage slipping away and couldn't bring myself to remove my clothing. I felt terribly out of place, as though I were naked in a room full of fully clad people.

Sauce Boy finished dumping a bucket of ketchup on a woman's behind and gestured for me to join in but I backed up toward the safety of the dining room as food flew everywhere—baked beans, fruit cocktail, maple syrup, ice cream and much more I couldn't identify. I lost track of Sauce Boy when he dove into a mound of green gelatin, shouting gleefully.

"Get in here!" yelled a woman I knew only as "Pudding Puss" but I backed up another step or two as a container of cottage cheese whizzed past my head. I wore a pantsuit I'd bought at Penney's only a week before and didn't want to ruin it.

It didn't matter. A voice came from behind me: "You're a shy one, aren't you?" Suddenly I found myself pushed into the midst of the food frenzy. Within seconds I was covered with goo, face-to-face with a naked woman smeared with gravy. She clutched her breasts and wiggled them at me provocatively, her eyes gleaming with lust. Fortunately, I was saved from an embarrassing encounter when she slipped on a chunk of margarine and fell into a group of people playing with cans of aerosol cheese.

The floor was ankle deep in food at that point. People threw in oatmeal, jelly (grape, I think), applesauce, and spaghetti and meatballs, a messy cornucopia covering the increasingly excited bodies of the participants. Since my pantsuit was ruined beyond repair, I let my hair down a little, so to speak, and got a little caught up in the spirit of the thing. Scrambling from the writhing masses, I found my own bookbag—from the Bluestocking Book Cellar, if you're interested—and removed a large can of peas. Obviously, I wasn't thinking clearly, as I forgot to open the can before I sailed it into the mob. It struck a man I knew as "Oozy Freddie" in the back of the head. He slumped to the floor and was quickly lost in the sploshing frenzy.

Taking a moment to catch my breath, I retrieved my other contribution, a restaurant-sized can of pickle brine.

Let me take a moment to defend myself. Not being an experienced splosher, I felt unsure of what to bring, but on my way to the party, I passed my cousin Milo's restaurant and inspiration struck. He happily gave me the huge jar of pickle brine, saying I had saved him the trouble of throwing it away. I sincerely thought the brine, being slimy and pungent, would be a welcome addition to the proceedings. I really did.

Back at the party, I opened the jar and emptied the pickle brine on my fellow revelers. This turned out to be unfortunate because moments before, several sploshers had dumped dozens of boxes of baking soda into the fray. It gave the proceedings an attractive wintry look but as I discovered to my horror, pickle brine mixed with baking soda results in *foam*. Lots and lots of foam, rapidly expanding to the point where it becomes hard to breathe. I watched, stunned, as the sploshers disappeared in a throbbing green cloud of goop.

Like a living thing, the roiling blob quickly burst from the living room, spreading toward the rest of the house. Frightened shouts filled my ears as people screamed, "What's going on?" and "Help! I can't see!" I retreated, numb with shock, as the occasional head or limb emerged from the thick foam, only to disappear again.

Acting on instinct, I grabbed my purse and ran to the back of the house, the giant globule at my heels. Escaping through the kitchen door, I hurried to my car, not caring what my food besmirched clothing did to the upholstery. As the engine roared to life, I took a glance at the house. The foam had risen to cover the windows, blocking out the light from inside, with more ooze squirting from under the back door, rolling down the steps into the yard. Hoarse shouts filled the air as I drove away, much embarrassed.

The newspaper ran a lengthy story the next day. Happily, no one was injured other than Oozy Freddie, who suffered a minor head contusion. Emotions, however, ran high. It seems that the foam spread to the entire house, crawling up the stairs to the second floor, where it reached a height of eight feet. At least a dozen ambulances and fire department vehicles were dispatched to the scene, administering oxygen to those who needed it.

Several of my host's neighbors were interviewed for the article, all of them complaining about the terrible stench emanating from the house and demanding that the authorities do something about it. My host was quoted as well, complaining about some "blonde nutjob who showed up out of nowhere with chemical weapons." I suppose he meant me. I can't blame him for being angry but personal insults are uncalled for. After all, my mission is only to serve science. Surely he would understand.

Hopefully the discussion in this chapter demonstrates some of the wide variety of fetishistic pursuits going on even as we speak. Think of it—somewhere, people are fondling pumpkins in a lewd way or dressing like a spider monkey as part of their sexual experience.

I was concerned I might develop a fetish of my own by becoming involved in such activities but this was not the case. I will continue to regard rubber gloves as cleaning helpers and nothing more, and I certainly have no desire to dress up like an ocelot or other wild creature. But if I never see a pickle again, it will be too soon.

Chapter Six

Lifestyles—How to live when no one is looking

DON'T WE ALL HAVE A LIFESTYLE?

Well, yes, but in the world of kink, *lifestyle* has a different meaning. You often hear kinky folks talk about "being in the lifestyle," or more specifically, they might boast of being in the lifestyle "24/7" or even "24/7/365". I suspect these numbers refer to some kinky instruction manual. For a moment, I thought they might be a secret satanic message, like those you get when you play Bee Gees albums backward. I'm pretty sure it's the Bee Gees. Maybe not. I vaguely recall a group that ran around on stage wearing devil hats and spitting on the spectators.

After a while, I remembered it was the number "666" that gets the satanic people in a froth, jumping up and down and screeching things from that *Exorcist* movie. So, none of that stuff has anything to do with kinky lifestyles, though I can't speak for the Bee Gees, since I don't have access to what they do behind closed doors.

My friend Amanda has a theory about this "24/7" business and she ought to know. Not only is she from New York City but her husband subscribes to *Playboy* magazine, so they may well be privy to information that does not reach the average citizen. According to Amanda, "24/7" means that a person practices a particular kink all the time, not even taking a breather for birthdays or Thanksgiving. It boggles the mind, and yet Amanda seems to know about these things. After all, she has a tattoo of an eagle, I believe it is, on the side of her ankle. I suspect she has an interesting history she's not talking about.

Up to this point I had assumed the majority of kinky behavior went on at night and on weekends, so the idea of people being nonstop kinky warranted further investigation. One wonders what these people do when they visit their mothers. "Oh yes, Mom, I got these marks across my face because Master Ironhead tied me to the wall and whipped me for several hours. We do it every day!" I don't know about your mother but mine would have a serious conniption fit.

Let's take a look at some common kinky lifestyles, shall we?

Female rule: In perusing Uncle Henry's kinky library, I noticed much of the material concerned women taking command and dominating males. In a world where most western societies are patriarchal in nature, a home where the woman rules the roost is kinky indeed, especially if the woman runs around in a leather catsuit cracking a whip.

Despite the popularity of female rule in kinky circles, I wasn't able to meet a woman who practiced this lifestyle until I was invited to appear—as Mistress Dominique—on a late-night radio program, *The Other Side*. Happily, the other guest that night was a woman known as Rowena the HypnoDomme, who told me she was a lifestyle dominatrix with six fulltime male slaves living under her roof.

Sitting in the radio studio, Rowena didn't strike me at first glance as a domme. She dressed in a pair of jeans, a simple white cotton top and stained sneakers. Physically, there was nothing remarkable about her except for the dark green eyes bulging from her face, almost frog-like. It was hard to keep from staring at them but that probably works to her advantage, being a hypnotist and all.

Reproduced below is a transcript of the interview conducted by the host of the radio program, a man known as Big Bob Burgess:

Burgess: Welcome back to The Other Side, the program that looks at the strange, the bizarre, the sleazy underbelly of what we call life. Tonight I have two guests who might scare some of our male listeners. They call themselves dominatrixes but I call 'em hookers. In the studio are Mistress Dominique and her fellow prostitute, Rowena the HypnoDomme. Welcome to the show, ladies.

Mistress Dominique: What? I am not a prostitute!

Burgess: It's the twenty-first century, babe! Be proud you're a sex worker. How about you, Rowena? You like walking the streets?

Rowena: Look into my eyes, Big Bob Burgess. What do you see?

Burgess: We'll get to that in a moment, babe. First, I want to ask Mistress Dominique about her interesting outfit. Of course, you can't see this at home but Dominique is wearing a green terrycloth bathrobe with blue…uh, daisies embroidered on it. And lime green platform sandals. What's up with that, Dominique?

MD: Well, I know some men have a fixation of being dominated by a geisha. As kimonos are rather hard to come by here, I had to make do with what I had at hand.

Burgess: Ah. I've never seen a blonde geisha before. And you have…uh, looks like birds stuck in your hair.

MD: Yes. Plastic birds.

Burgess: Okay. Hey, we've got a caller on line one. Go ahead, caller.

Caller: Annabelle? Is that you? This is your mother. Ruth called and said you were on the radio telling everyone you're a prostitute. You stop that right now!

MD: Mother! I did not say I'm a prostitute. The radio man said it.

Caller: I can't believe you're making a spectacle of yourself like this! What's gotten into you?

Rowena: Listen to the sound of my voice, Annabelle's mother. I have captured your soul.

Burgess: So you don't like your daughter, or should I say, Mistress Dominique, standing on street corners wearing a bathrobe?

Caller: I should say not! We're good Presbyterians. If we were Lutherans, well, that's another story, but we're not!

MD: Mother, I don't hang out on street corners wearing a bathrobe and I'm not a prostitute.

Rowena: Annabelle's mother. Give in to me. Your soul is mine.

Caller: Shut up, you tart! I'm talking to my daughter.

MD: Mother, hang up. I'll explain when I get home.

Caller: We'll see about that.

Burgess: All lines are open! Give us a call, you freaks and perverts! Now, Rowena, I understand that you turn men into your willing slaves by hypnotizing them, right?

Rowena: Yes. Even now, you feel your will giving itself over to my demands.

Burgess: Sure. Could you back up a little? You need to keep your chair near the microphone. Thanks. These men that you hypnotize—are they your slaves all the time or do you charge them by the hour?

Rowena: Once I capture their souls, they belong to me forever. They worship me, just as you will, Bob Burgess.

Burgess: Wow. You must not get much repeat business. You brought one of your slaves to the studio tonight, is that right?

Rowena: Yes.

Burgess: You might want to give him another dose of the ol' hypnotic stare. I saw him flirting with Connie the receptionist.

Rowena: Impossible! His will belongs to me.

Burgess: Okay. Now Mistress Dominique, are you a (laughs) professional geisha?

MD: Actually, I'm working on an ethnographic study of kinky practices.

Burgess: That's interesting. Rowena, could you back away a little? That stare is getting on my nerves.

Rowena: Your will is strong but soon it will be mine.

Burgess: Whatever. Dominique, what is a…what did you call it? An ethnological study?

MD: Ethnographic. It's a form of research in which I involve myself with the subjects under study.

Burgess: And, of course, that requires you to stand on street corners in a bathrobe.

MD: Certainly not. I am merely adopting a clothing style favored by kinky people.

Burgess: You could take a clue here, Rowena. I mean, there's nothing wrong with your outfit but it's not all that—okay, I'm going to have to ask you to back away again. It's really creeping me out. How do get your eyes to bug out like that?

Rowena: You feel your soul helplessly drifting into my domain, Bob Burgess. Don't fight it. Let it happen.

Burgess: Yeah. How many slaves do you have at the moment?

Rowena: There are six who serve me. You will make the seventh.

Burgess: Hey, another caller. Go ahead, you're on The Other Side!

Caller: Annabelle? It's your mother again. I thought you said you were coming home. You're still on the radio!

MD: In a minute, okay? I'm doing research here.

Burgess: Gotta go, Mom, we've got a caller on line two. Talk to me!

Caller: Yeah, that chick in the bathrobe. What's she charge for a sixty-nine?

Burgess: Mistress Dominique? How much for a sixty-nine?

MD: Nothing! I don't charge because I'm not—

Caller: It's free? Wooooohoooo! Yeah!

Burgess: You'll never get rich that way. Let's get back to Rowena. You're in charge of six slaves—what's an average day like for you?

Rowena: I do what I want. My slaves take care of my every need. Just as you will, Bob Burgess.

Burgess: So, you don't have to mow the lawn, rake the leaves, no cooking, cleaning, right?

Rowena: You will do that for me.

Burgess: Okay, seriously. Back the chair away and sit where you're supposed to or out you go. Speaking of going out, looks like your slave just walked out the door with Connie.

Rowena: No! I'll kill the bastard!

Burgess: Well, Rowena just charged out of the studio. (laughs) I wouldn't want to be in that slave's shoes. And here's another caller. Speak to me!

Caller: Annabelle? This is Aunt Ruth. Your mother called and she's having fits about you turning into a prostitute. I love ya, hon, but you better come home. I know you haven't found steady work as an academic but something will come along. You don't have to give it away. Hey, stop that, Carlos. Stop it! I'm on the phone! Ohhhh, lord. Okay, gotta go. See you soon!

MD: Aunt Ruth? Tell Mother I'm not a prostitute!

Burgess: Sorry, she's gone. Will you be working the streets tonight? Must get chilly, wearing only a bathrobe.

MD: Oh, that's it. Goodbye.

There was hell to pay with my family for weeks afterward and I'm not sure I ever got it through anyone's head that I'm not a prostitute. I did try to follow up on Rowena the HypnoDomme but when I went to the address she gave me, I found a small, ramshackle house not far from the railroad tracks. The man who answered the door was drunk as a skunk and when I asked if Rowena was there, he laughed and grabbed at my chest. Over his shoulder, I saw a wild party in progress, with a dozen men and women in various stages of undress. A beer keg sat in the middle of the living room, dripping on the carpet.

When the man at the door made another drunken lunge at me, I fled for the car. As I drove away I saw a woman struggling to mow the backyard with an ancient lawn mower. For a second I thought it was Rowena but surely a woman with her powers wouldn't be mowing the yard on such a hot afternoon and she certainly wouldn't let anyone chain her to the mower like that.

Gor: In packing away Uncle Henry's things, I discovered several science fiction novels about a planet called Gor. There are apparently quite a few of these Gor books, with titles such as *The Carpools of Gor, The Insurance Agents of Gor, The Hippies* *of Gor*, and so on. I skimmed one of them to get an idea of what they were about. Apparently, Gor is a planet ruled by a race of bug people, cockroaches or ants, insects of some sort. Despite being bugs, they are quite intelligent and able to build spacecraft that take them to Earth, where they kidnap people and take them back to Gor. As far as I can tell, the Gors eat some of their victims, as giant insects are wont to do, and make slaves of those who appear to be most fit for work in the filth mines. It's not clear exactly what's in the mines but since bugs like filth, it seems reasonable to assume that the Gors would want to collect as much filth as possible without having to actually touch it any more than necessary.

Clearly, these Gor books are nothing like more popular science fiction fare such as *Star Trek*. Usually, when Captain Kirk encountered bug people, he'd have Mr. Spock blow them up with a space phaser. That seems like a more fitting end to giant, slimy insectoids but the existence of the Gor books is evidence there is an audience for bug creatures that don't end up squished underfoot or sprayed with insecticide.

How this relates to kinky lifestyles is that in the Gor subculture, all of the insect men are masters and all the Earth women their slaves, so it's like a whole planet of S&M. However, I should note that *The Interior Decorators of Gor* mentions a band of fierce warrior Gor women who terrorize the Gor men to the point where the men refuse to live in anything but walled cities. Good for them! The women, I mean.

But here's the interesting lifestyle part—there are actually people who model their lives after these books, right down to the last detail. There are even numerous Internet groups that discuss how a person can completely immerse themselves and their partners in the Gor world of space aliens, filth mines and forced servitude. Is that wacky or what?

The idea of people emulating the denizens of a bug planet intrigued me. Happily, I unexpectedly ran into some Gors at the local comic book shop, where I'd gone to get a birthday gift for my nephew Chip, who's quite the fan of Batman. I keep hearing that Batman and his young colleague Robin have some sort of gay relationship. I didn't notice this while watching any of the Batman movies but perhaps I wasn't paying enough attention. It's a sad thing to hear about Batman, whom I thought was a good role model for our youth.

Anyway, I found several young men hanging around the comic book store and I noticed a couple of them wore t-shirts emblazoned with the covers of Gor novels. I also noticed the young men were similar in appearance, being in various stages of obesity that their colorful t-shirts did little to disguise. Also, they seemed in need of a good dermatologist due to the nasty acne condition from which they all suffered.

I moved a little closer and saw the young men huddled around a Gor novel. One of them read aloud in a cracked voice, stopping when one of the others snickered or made a crude comment about the female slaves depicted in the story. When one of the young people returned from a visit to the facilities, I managed to waylay him long enough to have a short discussion. He identified himself with his Gor name, Billy of Hoohah, or something like that. It was hard to understand any of the youngsters, as they constantly ate candy and tried to talk with their mouths full.

In his Gor persona, which he expresses only on the Internet, Billy lives in the walled city of Skiin Aulus, where he owns twelve slave women. According to Gor law, he told me with a smirk, these women must give him sex whenever he demands it.

As it turns out, he only knows these women via email communication. After much prodding, Billy admitted he'd never had a girlfriend or even gone on a date, much less had a sexual encounter. This admission caused him to blush with embarrassment and before I could ask any further questions, Billy scuttled off to rejoin his friends. For a moment, the thought passed that I might fix him up with my cousin Jenna's daughter, Cassie, but I suspected Cassie wouldn't want to date anyone who pretends to be from a bug planet.

The most interesting facet of the Gor lifestyle, as depicted in the novels, is a specific code of conduct based on the premise that men are the masters of women. In order to preserve their superior status, the bug overlords of the planet enforce strict rules regarding clothing. Women are required to wear leather collars symbolic of their lowly status and, if they're clothed at all, are allowed to wear only scraps of cloth that do little to provide any warmth or protection. Of course, scanty clothing also makes the women easily accessible to the men, which is certainly no treat for any woman with a sense of modesty. I mentioned this clothing rule to a female neuropsychologist of my acquaintance, Susan von Aught, who grimaced and made the following comment:

This business of dressing women in rags is obviously an aspect of a male fantasy world, a place where men can practice avoidance of their fear of shopping with women. In addition, it is a place where they can give full rein to the little boy within them who can't stand to wait while a woman gets dressed. How better to resolve these fears than take away women's clothing? What a bunch of dorks!

It's no surprise that the male kinksters who practice the Gor lifestyle dress in a more elaborate fashion than the women. Since Gor is a planet of bug people, it's likely they dress in some sort of insect costume. One gets the image of women dressed in rags running away from giant insects clicking their mandibles, waving their antennae in a menacing fashion and making weird screeching noises, or however it is that insects communicate.

When you think about it, if the women of Gor had any brains at all, they would arm themselves with large flyswatters or rolled up newspapers, those items being the natural enemies of creepy crawly things, at least in my house. Or perhaps there is a planet Terminex populated by a race of exterminators who could help the Gor women by spraying the planet or setting out giant ant traps or whatever. But they don't and that gives us yet another kinky mystery that may never be resolved.

In addition to the clothing requirements, Gors seem to be keen on regimented behavior. A primary example of this is the way Gor women are kept subservient by learning a complex system of commands. Upon hearing such a command, the woman is required to contort her body in a specific position without any hesitation. Failure to do so, one presumes, would result in being eaten or thrown in the filth mines.

I learned about these positions during a phone interview with a middle-aged man known to his Gor comrades as Thaddius of Goom or some such thing. Communication was made difficult by Thaddius' insistence on cramming food in his mouth during our phone chat and by his mother's frequent yelling for Thaddius to take out the garbage. I did the best I could, given the circumstances, to transcribe his remarks as accurately as possible. According to Mr. Goom, some of the primary positions females must assume are:

Bara: She lays on her belly, her forehead pressed to the floor, trying not to notice the used gum in which Master has stepped. She crosses her ankles and places her wrists in the small of her back and waits to be bound.

Gor bow: She kneels, her thighs spread wide. She leans over backwards until she topples over and smacks her head on the floor. Rubbing the sore spot with her left hand, she gets up, leans forward until her head touches the floor and places her hands over her ears, so as not to hear Master's constant burping. She then pulls herself up, arches her back and exposes her breasts deliciously for her Master's enjoyment, for Master really likes to look at her boobage.

Hair: She remains in whatever position she is in at the time but gathers up her hair and offers it to Master, who has a real hair fetish thing going on.

Lesha: She stands, her back to her Master, with her feet exactly 6.7 inches apart, her wrists crossed at the small of her back, so she can get at that itch that's been bothering her all day. She holds her head high, turning it to her left, then to the right, fakes turning it back to the left, then stops. Her lips are slightly parted, tongue extended as far as it will go so she can make that cool motorboat sound Master so loves. Finally, she rolls her eyes in a gesture of exasperation and awaits his leash.

Nadu: She kneels with her thighs spread wide for Master's pleasure, her back arched elegantly, her head held high with eyes lowered submissively. She lays her hands on top of her head and says "Nadu, nadu," like the alien guy on *Mork and Mindy*.

Slave Lips: She turns her head up to Master, eyes closed, lips puckered as she does so. She waits motionless, forbidden to move even a muscle, until Master's kiss releases her or she gets bored and goes shopping.

Walk: When this command is given, the slave turns oh so gracefully, her long hair caressing her body as she turns. She walks quietly across the room or camp, putting her left foot in and her right foot out, then doing the hokey-pokey until Master tells her to quit fooling around.

Sula: Also known as the Sitting Position. The slave sits in front of a complicated looking console and steers a starship around. While in this position, the slave must respond to Master by saying "Aye, Captain" or "Warp three, Captain."

Ko-Lar: This position is apparently named after Superman's father or somebody from that Krypton planet. The slave assumes this position by pinning a towel around her neck so that it sort of looks like a cape then sticks her arms straight out in front and runs around the house making that *whhoooosh!* sound that people make when they do that.

I wasn't able to learn much else about Gors. They are a secretive bunch and though I asked to chat with several Gors I met online, they all tended to exhibit the same behavior—they'd issue me an order, I'd tell them to stuff it and they'd disappear. I thought about trying to infiltrate their ranks by posing as a scantily clad slave girl but the thought of men in bug costumes made me decide it wasn't worth it.

Goths: If you were to visit our local mall, the Crowne Pointe Centre, you would see some odd looking specimens hanging out at the food court, sipping Orange Juliuses while staring forlornly at the other patrons. It's easy to tell at a glance that these people belong to some sort of group—they dress alike, completely in black and wear similar makeup consisting of white face powder with terribly overdone mascara and loud red lipstick that simply isn't appropriate for daytime wear. Some have little Celtic symbols on their faces. All of them have jet-black hair but I suspect in most cases the color comes from a bottle. This look isn't only for the girls, mind you, but the boys as well.

These youngsters are quite a sight, clumped together in the food court, looking like those zombies you often see stumbling out of graveyards in bad horror films. They sound like zombies, too, going on and on in droning voices about how horrible life is, and how much pain we all suffer, and how there's no hope for anyone because everything will turn out awful no matter what anyone does. Some attitude.

As it turns out, the people hanging out at our mall are Goths, a relatively new subculture that isn't restricted to

Crowne Pointe Centre but can be found at malls across the country. When I first saw a pack of Goths, I thought they might be an odd mime troupe or perhaps a group of clown trainees who hadn't mastered the correct costuming or makeup. Getting an "F" in clown makeup class might explain their dour expressions but that isn't it. Goths are people who spend their lives being horribly depressed on purpose. They enjoy being "bummed out," as the kids say, and they've evolved an entire lifestyle and mode of personal grooming to perpetuate their depression.

Are Goths kinky? Of course they are. One look at those black clothes, the heavy black boots, the multitude of facial piercings and the makeup, and you can't avoid the conclusion that this is a kinky culture. But what kind of social structure do they have? They all look much the same, so from a distance it was hard to tell which Goths were dominant and which were submissive. I had to find out for myself, so I put on my ethnography hat and decided to gain access to the Goths. Of course, I'm not being literal when I refer to an ethnography hat. There's no such thing, as far as I know, and I can't imagine anyone running around wearing a hat with "ethnographer" emblazoned on it. No one could infiltrate a subculture wearing such a thing. It's a silly idea. I'm sorry I brought it up.

I must confess that I approached this situation with some trepidation. Okay, quite a bit of trepidation, so I took along Jim, one of the men who collect my trash. He is extremely muscular from picking up garbage cans all day and assured me that if any of the Goths tried anything rough, he would "squeeze their pointy little heads until their brains leaked out of their ears." Gross, yes, but reassuring. After all, we're talking about people who look like the Grim Reaper's fan club. For all I knew, they went around sucking blood out of people's necks or decapitating badgers under the full moon. In the end, I reminded myself that an ethnographer must be strong as well as scholarly, so I made my way to the food court.

Of course, I dressed the part. I don't own many black clothes but I managed to put together an appropriate outfit consisting of black rayon slacks, a black sweater and one of those furry black Russian hats I found in the back of the closet. Lord knows where it came from. I also put on more makeup than usual including a pair of heavy false eyelashes. Unfortunately, one of them fell off in the car and I couldn't find it, so I had to hope no one would notice.

Purchasing an Orange Julius, I sat nervously at a table near the Goths and watched them carefully, looking for suitable interview subjects. Finally, I screwed up my courage and approached a Goth couple and after I agreed to buy them each a hot pretzel with mustard, they agreed to talk. Their names are Mystryss Death Hole and Lucifer Nightshade Hell. My goal, by the way, was to interview both a male and female Goth. I'm reasonably sure that's what I did.

Mistress Dominique: Not only are you wearing unique outfits but you have interesting names as well.

Mystryss Death Hole: In order to express the beloved darkness that permeates my soul, I rejected the name my parents attempted to force upon me. My new name is a mirror into the blackness that envelops me.

MD: What was your original name?

Mystryss: It isn't important. That name is dead, gone to Valhalla.

MD: Oh, come on. It can't be that awful. How about another Orange Julius?

Mystryss: All right. It doesn't matter anyway. My name before I entered the beloved netherworld was, um, Heather.

MD: That's a cute name! Why couldn't you be Heather Death Hole?

Mystryss: I reject all that has to do with those who live in the sunshine! I am Mystryss Death Hole and will be forever more!

MD: Okay, dear, it was just a thought. Now, your friend here also has an interesting name.

Lucifer Nightshade Hell: I am Lucifer Nightshade Hell, lord of all that is dark and sinister and master of the portal into hell itself.

MD: I see. Would this be your occupation then?

Lucifer: My dark being is totally devoted to the desires of those who reign in darkness and pestilence.

MD: I'm confused. Does this involve a salary? Or are you still in school?

Lucifer: School? To be indoctrinated in the ways of the daytime dwellers? I think not!

MD: But do you have a job?

Lucifer: (pauses) Yes, my parents have inflicted the ways of the nonbelievers on me. I work…I work at Higgins Hardware. But I reject their mundane hardware and all it stands for!

MD: That's nice. So, what makes you a Goth?

Mystryss: I am Goth because I have discovered the path of misery and pain. I am a true child of the dark who has been allowed to know the full meaning of despair. I am shunned by those who live in the light and I revel in my lonely, brutal existence.

Lucifer: I am Goth because I like wearing makeup. Especially mascara. I love mascara!

Mystryss: What? Makeup? You can't love anything except misery and death!

Lucifer: Hey, makeup is fun! You know, my favorite part of the day is sitting in front of my makeup mirror, putting on a Barry Manilow CD and making myself look all Gothy and pretty.

Mystryss: Pretty? Goth is not about being pretty! We wear the look of those who embrace the netherworld!

Lucifer: It's a nice look. I've been thinking of switching to a more natural look for daytime wear but I think the paler shades are nice for a dramatic nighttime look and—

Mystryss: Did you say you listened to Barry Manilow? Barry Manilow? Of all men, he is Satan's enemy! His kind threaten all that is dark and hellish!

Lucifer: Well, I like him. He has a nice voice and his songs make me feel good.

Mystryss: Goths do not feel good! We travel the unlit trail of despair and sorrow!

Lucifer: Well, I have to go. There's a big sale down at the Gap. (He leaves at this point.)

Mystryss: Aaaarrrgh!

MD: We're getting a little off the track here. Aside from being depressed and dressing in a strange way, how is Goth kinky? Do Goths have sex?

Mystryss: Yes, we have sex but we make sure not to enjoy it. Such pleasures of the flesh are not for those who dwell in the shadows.

MD: I had the impression that Goth sex might involve a coffin and some fake blood, maybe a few chains?

Mystryss: That's only for posers like that rat bastard Lucifer. I should call him Stew because that's his name. Little Stewie, who likes to romp with the sun people. Rotten little—

MD: Let's stay with the sex thing. What is Goth sex? How is it kinky?

Mystryss: Goth sex is painful, a dreary meeting of two tortured souls uniting their bodies to share the unbearable pain and sorrow of life.

MD: You sound like my cousin Helen. She just got divorced last week. Thank you for your time, Mystryss Death Hole. I hope things get better for you.

Mystryss: I don't.

Ponyplay: I discovered this lifestyle by accident one day, when I went to the feed store to buy a bag of birdseed. This feed store sells a bit of everything, including horse tack. I've never ridden a horse but out of curiosity I wandered to the equine section to see what all was involved in taming such a powerful beast. The first thing I spotted was a rack full of riding crops and whips. Aha! I said to myself. This feed store sells bondage equipment on the side. It's no wonder they've been in business for so long.

As it turns out, that wasn't exactly the case. However, as I wandered the equine section, checking to see if they sold handcuffs, I happened to overhear two men examining a display of leather harnesses.

"I wonder if this would fit Petunia," the first man said with a snicker.

"Still got your wife in the barn, eh?" asked the second man.

"Hell, yeah. She's been a pony six months. She loves it when I saddle her up and take her for a ride around the backyard. A real thoroughbred. Of course, I have to do all my own cookin' now. I don't like that much. But we don't spend any money on her clothes!"

The second man nodded in approval. "Sheila's a right good pony, too. You ought to hear her whinny when I get her tacked up."

At that point, both men turned and stared at me. In my desire to listen to their conversation, I had gotten too close and invaded their personal space. Stammering with embarrassment, I hastily explained my interest in their activities, which caused the men to laugh. "Sure, that's why you're here," said the first man, winking at me.

Despite my protestations, the men had decided I was into ponyplay. I realized this could open a door for my research, so I stopped quibbling with them and admitted I wanted nothing more than to be a pony. The men nodded at this, and the first man scribbled an address on the back of a business card. "Our next meeting is tomorrow night. Hope to see you there, filly." Then they laughed and walked away.

That night, I did some hurried research on the Internet and discovered that ponyplay is a popular pursuit, with pony clubs scattered all over the country. Membership appears to be split between those whose kink involves being trained as a pony and those adopt the role as a pony trainer.

As is always the case with kinky endeavors, there is an enormous amount of hardware involved, almost all of it bondage devices. A human pony is outfitted much like an equine, with reins, a harness, a collar, blinders, a bit, a saddle and, most interestingly, a tail. All of this equipment is designed to give the trainers control over the ponypersons, who are not allowed to talk or use their hands.

Further research showed that kinky ponies enjoy this bondage but perhaps even more, they enjoy putting aside their human personas and dropping into **ponyspace**, a mindset in which they trade the intellect and rationality of a human for the primal and impulsive behavior of a beast. That idea bothered me, as I couldn't imagine putting my trained brain to rest and acting on instinct. However, that wouldn't be required, as I only needed the research experience of being around ponyplayers.

I arrived at the designated address the next evening, a ranch-style home in a rural area near a large forest. My host, a short paunchy man in a western outfit, introduced himself as "Wrangler Steve". One of the men I'd met at the feed store whispered into Wrangler Steve's ear and he smiled and led me to the barn, bypassing a table filled to overflowing with delicious appetizers. Spotting me eyeing the treats, Steve shook his head. "Ponies don't eat that sort of thing," he said. "You'll get a nice treat, don't you worry none."

Wrangler Steve had set up his expansive backyard as a corral, complete with a small red barn. Entering the barn, I got a whiff of fresh hay mixed with body odor from the stalls we passed, all but one holding nude women in full pony gear—harness, reins, saddle, the whole outfit.

Stopping in front of a stall, Steve pointed at a red-haired, overweight woman snoring on a bed of straw. "Used to be my wife," he said, grinning. "Now she's a pony fulltime. I call her Fireball." The woman snorted in her sleep and rolled over, letting loose with a loud fart. "That's my Fireball!" Steve said with a laugh.

I was led to the empty stall, where a man who called himself "Wild Bill Cock" waited. This is where events went wrong. Before I knew it, Steve pinned my arms behind my back while Wild Bill strapped a harness to my head. He was adept at his work and quickly had a spoon bit stuck in my mouth. I protested mightily when he began removing my clothing but all that came out of my mouth were guttural noises as the spoon bit pressed down on my tongue. I then struggled to free my arms but Wrangler Steve held me easily. "She's a wild one, ain't she?" Bill said. "We'll have fun tamin' this filly." He looked in my eyes. "Maybe you'll be like our other ponies—most of 'em ain't had clothes on in years."

Despite my gurgled protests, I soon found myself naked and blushing furiously. The men imprisoned my hands in gloves that looked like hooves, then bound the hooves behind my back. When I continued to struggle, Bill pushed me down into the straw lining the stall. He quickly slid knee-length leather boots over my feet, forcing them to assume a position as if I were wearing extremely high heels. The reason for this, I quickly realized, was that the bottom of the boots were also shaped like hooves, complete with heavy horseshoes.

Wild Bill laced the boots tight and smiled as he clipped a pair of blinders to my harness, severely limiting my vision. "This palomino ain't got no tail," he said to the other man, who snickered.

What happened next was possibly the most degrading thing I have ever experienced. After rolling me on my stomach, one of the men smeared a glob of cold, gooey stuff on my behind, and then, to my utter horror, he shoved a butt plug into my nether region. I felt hair brushing against the back of my legs and knew I had been outfitted with a tail.

At that point, I lost my temper and began thrashing in the stall but to no avail. The men put hobbles on my ankles, leaving me with limited mobility. I howled into the bit, demanding to be freed but the men laughed and said I needed to work on my whinny. Then they helped me to my feet and strapped a bag of oats on my harness. I was left alone.

As I stood in the stall, my nose filled with the odor of the slightly moldy oats, my fury eventually faded. Okay, so they've got me, I decided. I'll go along with it. I'll get terrific research material and…well, I didn't know what else. A calm descended on me and I felt myself drifting, perhaps into ponyspace.

A while later, Wild Bill returned. "I plumb forgot to give you a name," he said, wrinkling his brow in thought as his eyes zeroed in on my bosom. "I think I'll call you *Melon*." He nodded and snapped a lead to my harness. "Come on, Melon. Time to start your training."

I walked gingerly in the hoof boots out of the barn to a corral, to join several other women in the same getup as mine. They held their heads tall as they pranced with high steps in cadence. Giving me a whack on the behind, Will Bill urged me to join them. I hesitated for a moment and then decided to follow orders and let my inner equine out. Falling in behind the other ponies, I attempted to prance in the cruel boots but they were heavy and running on tiptoe was no treat.

Things went fine for a little while but then I tripped as I passed Wild Bill. He snarled and lashed out with a whip, catching me on the back of the thigh.

"Now, that's too much!" I mumbled from under the bit.

"Get moving, you nag!" Steve yelled, catching me again with the whip.

He can't tame a wild pony like me, I told myself. I yearn to run free!

Whinnying loudly, I broke ranks and stomped my right hoof on Bill's hand-tooled cowboy boot. He let out a scream, followed by language that would make a sailor blush.

"You stupid haybag! I'll show you who's boss!" he yelled, whacking me yet again.

A red mist rose before my eyes and cold fury filled my soul. Before I realized it, I had kicked Wild Bill in the stomach, sending him sprawling. The other ponies watched, whinnying encouragement, their eyes wide with excitement. Suddenly they all broke loose, stampeding around the corral. It turned into a mob scene—whips cracking, orders shouted, hooves thundering and screams of pain, mostly from the trainers.

The other ponies, following my lead, had tasted freedom, and they liked it. They also discovered the kicking power of their hooves. Some tried kicking backward, which gave them even more power. Before long, trainers littered the ground, moaning in pain and clutching their stomachs. Wrangler Steve's pony, Fireball, began kicking at the wooden fence, smashing a large hole in it. She let out a loud whinny and the other ponies thundered through the hole toward the nearby woods and freedom.

I started to follow when a twinge of pain reminded me of the infernal device embedded in my rear. I aimed a particularly vicious kick at the nearest trainer and sent him face-first into the dirt.

At that point, new shouts erupted and I watched with horror as the Rocking Robins, a birding group of which I was treasurer, emerged from the woods. My pony thoughts disappeared as I remembered turning down an invitation some weeks ago to join them on an expedition to these woods. Praying they wouldn't recognize me, I put my head down and ran for the barn.

Once safely inside, I turned and watched the birders frantically fighting off the enraged ponies, who were apparently so deep in ponyspace that any human was fair game. Old Mr. Jenkins whacked at a brunette pony with his cane as she attempted to head-butt him. A tall blonde ponygirl, snorting and neighing, kicked at Gladys Northbottom, who threw her binoculars at the pony but missed. Gladys' husband, Burt, somehow ended up in Fireball's saddle, clinging to the reins as she bucked and farted. I'll have to give old Burt credit—he stayed in the saddle a long time before being thrown off and landing hard against a tree.

A hand grabbed me from behind and I turned to look into the blackened, swollen eyes of Wild Bill Cock. "Think you're running off with my expensive tack, do ya? Well, think again!" Shoving me to the floor, he removed the equine gear from my body. I suffered one last indignity as Bill roughly pulled the butt plug out of me with a loud *pop!* before he stalked away, muttering angrily.

I breathed a sigh of relief. I had my freedom but I had no clothes. My stall was empty except for my purse, so I put my brain into high gear, trying to think of a way to cover myself. Then I remembered—my raincoat was in the backseat. Yes! If I could only make it to the car! Grabbing my purse, I sprinted from the barn but as I ran around the corner of the house to where I'd parked, my dreams of avoiding trouble ended abruptly.

"Look!" shouted Gladys. "I told you this was Annabelle's car, but—" Her mouth dropped open as my nakedness registered.

"Holy hell!" said Warren Nussbaum. "I knew these people were up to no good. And that danged Annabelle's mixed up in it."

I stood and stammered, feeling a few wisps of straw fall from my hair. But try as I might, no words would form.

Margaret Edswanger walked up and stuck a trembling finger in my face. "If you think we're going to let some perverted nudist serve as treasurer of the Rocking Robins, think again! You're relieved of duty!"

I slunk to the car as the birders walked away. Thankfully, the raincoat was there, so I pulled it on and sat heavily behind the wheel, gazing at a corral in ruins. Very little of the fence still stood and the barn was rapidly being battered to pieces by the hooves of the ponygirls. Several trainers lay crumpled in the dust, crying out in pain, while the rest ran from the ponygirls, who were still intoxicated with their taste of freedom.

About a mile down the road, I had to slam on the brakes when a ponygirl broke through the shrubbery lining the road, a battered and bleeding trainer in pursuit. He caught her momentarily but she turned and gave him two hard kicks to the ribs. He sat down next to the road and vomited on himself.

I shook my head and drove around him. I'd had too much excitement for one day. And, I had to admit, there are some kinky behaviors I will never understand.

Chapter Seven

Finding Kink—It's out there, somewhere

ARE YOU THE ONLY ONE?

In the course of preparing this book, many people told me the same thing: "There must be something wrong with me. My desires are so strange! How could anyone else have the same weird turn-ons? I need help!"

Fear not, lonely kinkster. The chances are excellent that whatever rings your chimes will strike a similar chord with others, unless you're into something extra bizarre, like demanding that your wife dress up as Winston Churchill and deliver one of his more famous speeches whenever you have sex. (This is one of the strangest things I could think of but I know after this book comes out, I'm going to hear from a bunch of people with a Winston Churchill fetish. If you are one of them, please don't be offended.)

As I see it, your problem is finding kindred souls so you won't feel so strange and alone when you do that stuff your mother told you not to do. Don't fret, because this chapter is here to help! You will learn there's an amazing variety of people and kinks out there, doing things you couldn't begin to imagine. And when you become involved with your fellow kinksters, perhaps you'll even run into someone you know, which could be a happy coincidence or terribly embarrassing, depending on what you're into and whether or not the authorities catch you doing it.

So, where are your comrades in kink? Read on, dear reader, read on.

The Internet: Today, the Internet is a vast network linking hundreds of millions of computers. This was not always the case. Government scientists originally developed the Internet so that in the event of a nuclear war, bureaucrats would have a secure means to write each other about how awful it is to have a nuclear war. But as time went by and no nuclear wars occurred, the scientists and bureaucrats got bored and began sending out smutty emails and dirty jokes. This proved to be a popular pastime and soon the nation's phone lines hummed with thousands of sexually explicit messages.

Eventually, one of the scientists figured out how to encode pictures so they could be sent over the Internet as well. It's said that the first such picture was pornographic, a nude photograph of former Secretary of Agriculture Dan Glickman stepping out of the shower but there is no way to confirm or deny this.

The ability to send naughty pictures not only caused a dramatic increase in Internet traffic, it also caught the attention of people who were not scientists or bureaucrats. Reasoning it was unfair for the government to keep such a powerful means of transmitting pornography to themselves, these people found a way for anyone to tap into the Internet and share in the growing amount of smut crisscrossing the country at the speed of light.

In a short time, millions of people joined in the fun. Many of them set up websites where patrons could look at any sort of pictures they wanted. There were sites featuring women fondling small animals, sites with women dressed up in lewd versions of Star Trek uniforms, even web pages crammed with pictures of women licking each other in disgusting ways. As would be expected, many sites showed women taking their clothes off and there were even a few sites for Baptists showing women putting their clothes back on. It was a veritable cornucopia of naughty images.

Eventually, people tired of looking at pictures. They wanted to *talk* about their kinky obsessions, so a few industrious souls started chat rooms, newsgroups and mailing lists, enabling kinksters all over the world to meet others with similar interests. These developments took the Internet to staggeringly high levels of popularity as more people hooked their computers to the network. At that point, the scientists who created the Internet shrugged their collective shoulders and gave up on using it as they had originally intended. All they could do was hope that a nuclear war never occurred because using the Internet to look at pornographic pictures certainly wasn't going to do much good in that event.

Let's take a look at some of the ways kinksters find each other on the Internet:

Newsgroups: Harkening back to the earliest days of the Internet, newsgroups are a convenient way to meet others. The process is quite simple. Using newsgroup software, you search for groups that appeal to your interests, and once you find them, you can read the messages posted there and post your own thoughts if you desire. It's Supreme Court Justice Oliver Wendell Holmes' "marketplace of ideas" come to life, except Mr. Holmes probably didn't envision the marketplace including discussions about steel underwear and what kind of vibrating butt plug to use on a first date.

These days, specialization is the order of the day as people explore increasingly explicit kinks, as shown in this progression of an early newsgroup:

alt.sex.pictures

alt.sex.pictures.naked

alt.sex.pictures.naked.women

alt.sex.pictures.naked.women.headless

alt.sex.pictures.naked.women.headless.communist

Of course, newsgroups were a boon for kinksters, as new and exciting erotic ideas spread across the globe with the click of a mouse button. I remember the first newsgroup I joined, alt.sex.baking.secrets. Well, I do like to bake, brownies being my specialty. Unfortunately, of the hundreds of messages I received from this newsgroup each day, the vast majority were messages telling me how I could increase my penis size, develop my bust or obtain a better home mortgage rate. Come to think of it, I never did see any messages about sexy baking. Too bad.

Don't assume, however, that newsgroups limit themselves to naked women, as in the examples above. For those whose interests go beyond such things, some of the more recent newsgroups explore an ever-increasing variety of kinky topics, as in these examples:

alt.sex.kink.booger

alt.dead.porn.stars

alt.sex.aluminum

alt.sex.nasal-hair

alt.sex.with.chickens.whilst.wearing.rubber.knickers

alt.sex.sheep.baaa.baaa.baaa.moo

soc.sexuality.kink.carpet.remnants

net.sexuality.bondage.tooth.floss

net.sexuality.kink.herbert.hoover

Mailing lists*:* As far as I can tell, mailing lists are similar to newsgroups, the main difference being fewer unwanted ads about penis enlargement. Not surprisingly, there are thousands of lists devoted to kinky themes. In Chapter Six, I reproduced a segment of a mailing list dealing with kinky smells. For this chapter I wanted a different perspective, so I set out to pick the brain of a list owner. After checking many lists, I found one called *Scene Shop*. If you'll recall, kinksters like to refer to erotic episodes as *scenes*, so when I saw this list, I just knew it was right.

Unfortunately, membership for the *Scene Shop* was closed, so I can't give you an in-depth look at kinksters recounting their scenes. Happily, I was able to convince the list owner, Richard Dotty, to answer a few questions over the phone, though I must admit up front this wasn't my best interview, as Mr. Dotty wasn't as forthcoming as I hoped. Perhaps list owners are a secretive lot by nature.

Mistress Dominique: How did you become interested in conducting scenes?

Dotty: I guess it started in college. The theater group was doing a production of *Naked Lunch* and—

MD: Say no more. Can we assume that nudity plays an important role in your scenes?

Dotty: Well, not really. Last year I had a part in an Anton Chekhov play. There was some nudity.

MD: And this Chekhov, is he into nude scenes as well?

Dotty: Not as such. In fact, some of his plays have gorgeous costumes.

MD: Ah. So your scenes also involve costuming. What are we talking about, mostly leather and latex?

Dotty: Uh, no. In some cases, satin and perhaps even velvet, but mostly more common fabrics. Whatever is appropriate for the players.

MD: Of course. I've done some research on players. Do they use toys in their scenes?

Dotty: Toys? I wouldn't call them toys. Like any other production, we have props. In the Chekhov play, we used a couple of knives because the scene required them.

MD: Oh, so you're into hardcore play. Aren't you afraid the use of these toys will result in serious injury or death?

Dotty: Uh, I'm confused. Why do you keep talking about toys?

MD: Don't be coy, Mr. Dotty. You know what I mean—whips, handcuffs, Argentinean steel-tipped floggers, spreader bars, that sort of thing.

Dotty: I have to go now.

MD: Thank you for your time. Oh. I guess he hung up.

Chat rooms*:* Another good way to meet fellow kinksters is to visit a chat room. There are thousands catering to those of the kinky persuasion. Visiting a chat room is easy. Once you install the appropriate software, all you have to do is connect to a chat room and log in. You will be asked for your "nick," or nickname, a pseudonym that not only makes you anonymous, but can also be used to identify what particular aspect of kink most interests you. For example, a nick such as "MsWhip" identifies a female dominant while "rbbrlover" is someone who has a fetish for rubber. On the other hand, if your chat room colleagues include people with handles like "moosefkkr," "fbi_rules!" or "poopflinger," it might be a good idea to try elsewhere.

A recent visit to the Wet Panties chat site revealed an amazing variety of rooms, most of them with the dumbest names, like Hot Twats or Pud's BlowMe Palace. Many of the names were misspelled, such as CumSuckers Alley and Jizzum In the Hizzum. As I've said before, it's a shame our schools are doing such a poor job of teaching the fundamentals these days. At any rate, here are a few of the chat rooms I found:

Domming Women

Domming Men

Domming Men Who Dress Like Women

Domming Men Who Dressed Like Women Once but Didn't Like It

Dungeon of Torment

Dungeon of Hellish Torture

Dungeon of Indescribable Pain

Dungeon of Mild Discomfort

Martha Stewart's Bondage My Way

Mr. Hate's Dungeon of Cole Slaw Recipes

Satan's House of Bran

Lady Amanda's Chamber of Odd Smells

Sexy Susan's Slice of Hell

Catholic and Kinky but Feeling Really Guilty About It

Severe Anal Bondage

Not-Quite-So-Severe Anal Bondage

Marxist Toilet Slaves

Recently I visited a chat room under the non-de-plume, MissBehave. The following is a transcript of the discussion that ensued. I wish it had been a more educational experience.

Sysop: MissBehave is in the room. Welcome!

LeatherMike: There's a girl in here? Hey doll! Whassup?

mrStrange: Bend over baby your time has cum!

LeatherPete: Man, I'll bet you got big ones huh?

MasterBob: I like big ones!!!!!!!

MissBehave: Good evening. Thank you for the welcome.

pudmeister: Ever have a guy shoot all over those big ones?

mrStrange: Bend over baby your time has cum!

WooMan: Woo!

MissBehave: I'm not sure what you mean by "big ones".

AdmiralMike: Any pirates here? Man, the other day I got an email from some nutball writing a book about kink, and she wanted to know about my crew. Told her I was going to bust her a good one with a marlin spike. LOLOLOLOLOLOLOL!!!!!!!!

BigRod: MissBehave, RU really a girl or one of them guys that pretends to be one?

TheFreak: I seen big ones on TV last night.

WooMan: Woo!

pudmeister: Little ones suck. Not dick, tho, huh huh.

mrStrange: Bend over baby your time has cum!

MissBehave: I do feel a bit lost in this conversation, as I don't know what "big ones" are. Could someone please explain?

MasterBob: I went out once with a girl that had big ones. I bout creamed me jeans every time she bent over.

BigRod: Once I had a date. I thought it was a real girl but it was one of them transformers.

LeatherPete: Dude! They aren't transformers—their called transvestilites.

MissBehave: If you're referring to me, Mr. Rod, yes, I am an authentic female.

WooMan: Woo!

TheFreak: You got big ones or not?

LeatherMike: Right now I'm watching a porno and the chick has HUGE ONES!!!!!!! They're like the size of Volkswagons!!!!!

WooMan: Woo!

MissBehave: I was really hoping to enter into some enlightening discussion regarding kinky practices. I wish someone would tell me about "big ones".

pudmeister: I'd like to enter into something! ROTFLMAO!!!

mrStrange: Bend over baby your time has cum!

LeatherPete: How are you supposed to tell when they're a real chick or not? I don't want to go out with any transvestilites.

TheFreak: Man, the transvestilites gots dicks! Don't you know nothing?!!!!!!

MissBehave: I'm beginning to wonder if this was such a good idea after all.

LeatherMike: I jst spppuurted all ovr my keybaorrrd. Howww to claen it??&?

WooMan: Woo!

pudmeister: I saw on TV once this transvestilite got injections and grew big ones—really big ones.

LeatherPete: Injected what?

pudmeister: I don't know. Prolly grape jelly or silicone caulking compound.

TheFreak: They still gots dicks!!!!!

MissBehave: All right, this was a bad idea. Thank you very much for your time.

LeatherPete: Grape jelly would stink like hell after a while.

WooMan: Woo!

<<MissBehave has left the room>>

Clubs: The Internet, while a useful resource for kinksters, is certainly not the only option. Most large cities have at least one bondage club, a place where kinky people can congregate and engage in mutually satisfying activities. One of the most famous clubs in the world is the venerable Flaming Hellhole, catering to kinksters since 1977. Vicky, an old college chum of mine, remembers going there in the early 1990s:

We were in a silly mood that night. Our travel group had never been to New York City before and we decided to do something decadent. A couple of the men wanted to go to a strip club but most of the women thought that was disgusting, except, of course, for Evelyn. Anyway, somebody said it would be fun to go to one of those S&L or S&M places, I can't remember exactly what they're called. There was all kinds of quibbling about it but finally that's what we decided to do. I was sure we'd all end up getting arrested but I'd had a second glass of chardonnay with dinner, so I wasn't as cautious as I should have been.

We piled into a cab and drove around forever, it seemed, until the cabbie let us off in front of what he said was the best bondage club in the city. He was a strange duck, laughing his head off as he drove away. Evelyn ran into the street and gave him the finger, but I don't know why.

Well, we stood in front of this strange looking place, all painted in black except for a little red sign with the name of the club on it. There were all kinds of weird people hanging around, laughing and spitting on each other. If someone spit on me I'd be upset, but these people seemed to like it! Just stood there, laughing and spitting like there was no tomorrow. We made sure to stand well away from them.

That wasn't the only strange thing. They had such crazy hairstyles, when they had any hair at all. A lot of the women – at least I think they were women – were bald, and the men had spiky hair or one of those Mohawk Indian things with just a tuft of hair running down the middle of their head. And horrible clothes, all ripped up like they'd got their outfits out of a trashcan.

I don't know what kind of parents these people had, but obviously they weren't very good at parenting. The women looked positively scandalous! They wore far too much makeup and the ones that had hair wore it in ridiculous colors like purple or green. Green! And some of them had safety pins in their noses! That can't be sanitary!

Well, you wanted to know about the club. We finally screwed up our courage and went inside. I couldn't believe how loud it was! They played horrible music that sounded like a bunch of drunken chimps had gotten a hold of guitars and a leaf blower. You know, I can stand a little rock and roll, but this was too much. It hurt my fillings. We stood against the back wall to get away from the clamor as much as possible.

The other people in the club seemed to think the awful racket was wonderful. I've never seen such gyrating in my life, like a meeting of all the people in the world who can't dance – some of them were so awful that they kept banging into other people. Come to think of it, that happened a lot. It must have hurt like the dickens but I don't remember anyone getting angry about it.

There were other people who jumped up and down like they were on a pogo stick. If I did that I'd probably upchuck, but these people just kept going, up and down, up and down. There was no way I was going on that dance floor, no way. Besides, we hadn't seen any of that bondage stuff that everyone was so keen about. All I could make out was this huge clump of people, banging into each other and spitting.

I turned to ask Evelyn if she could spot any of those whips and chains the bondage people are supposed to use, but she was gone. I finally spotted her on the dance floor, hopping like it was the end of the world and waving her blouse over her head. I couldn't believe it!

I guess the bondage people liked her – they were spitting on her like crazy and she spit right back. At that point we decided enough was enough and it was time to leave, but we couldn't get Evelyn off the dance floor. She'd taken off her nice tweed skirt and was bumping heads with a woman dressed in a garbage bag. We had to leave without her. I don't know how she got back to the hotel.

So, that was my evening at the Flaming Hellhole. It was a letdown. I expected to see people dressed in leather and waving whips and chains around, but it was mainly badly dressed people with awful haircuts spitting and running into each other. Guess I don't have to worry about being a pervert. It didn't look like fun at all!

BDSM groups: Kinksters in many cities have formed local organizations promoting that voodoo that they do so well, or words to that effect. A quick search of the Internet revealed many such groups, a few of which are listed below:

Tied to Be Fit (A kinky fitness group?)

Thanks for the Spanks

Greater Chicago Eat, Meet and Beat

North Carolina Bondage and Mobile Home Maintenance Club

Cuffs 'n Stuff

Fetish Fiends!

Hanky Spanky of Cleveland, Inc.

Northeast Pittsburgh Chapter, T3WD

The "T3WD" acronym in the name of the latter group puzzled me. I saw it repeatedly while conducting my research but never found out what it stood for. One day I sat down with a pad of legal paper, a pencil and a dictionary, determined to figure it out. After several hours I came up with "Torrid Trombonists Trembling with Desire." I'm awfully good with word games and such, but to be honest, I'm not sure I got it right. Some aspects of the kinky lifestyle remain murky, even to me.

Most kinky groups hold monthly meetings, called **munches**. These meetings are usually held at a restaurant where the pervy crowd can dine while discussing the latest torture technology and other important matters. I wasn't aware that munches were held in my area until I perused the "Out and About" section of the newspaper and saw that a group was meeting at a nearby Red Lobster to discuss "Of Human Bondage." Of course, the ethnographer in me couldn't let such a golden opportunity pass by.

What I didn't know at the time is that because munches are held in public, kinky attire is frowned upon. Unfortunately, I arrived at the Red Lobster clad in a fetish outfit I'd hurriedly put together, consisting of a battered red leather coat I'd found at a thrift shop, a cowboy hat, white patent leather platform boots and a tight purple dress with thigh-high slits I'd borrowed from Stacey, my divorcée friend from down the street. Oh, and fishnet hose. Stacey insisted on it. "You won't catch any fish without the right bait," she purred. I tried to tell her that I hated fishing but she wouldn't listen.

The folks in the Of Human Bondage group held their munch in a private room at the back of the restaurant, where they were seated around a long table. I tried to be discreet as I entered, but it was not to be. Everyone in the restaurant gawked and pointed at me. My reception in the private room was no better, as the group had worn conservative attire, dark suits and flower print dresses and so forth, so I stuck out like a sore thumb.

I tried to fit in by joining the table chatter. Turning to the prim, silver-haired woman on my left, who didn't look even a bit kinky, I asked her how long she'd been a bondage fan. "Many years," she said, smiling. "Maugham is truly the master." I blinked in shock. I'd run across many kinky groupings during my research, but never a mother dominating a daughter, at least not in a kinky sense.

"Mom is the master?" I repeated. "Does Mom use whips on you? Does she put you in restraints?"

The woman looked at me in horror. "What a terrible thing to say!"

I nodded. "I understand. She must use more intimate pain implements, such as nipple clamps. Or a butt plug, perhaps?"

"Butt plugs?" The woman's eyes grew as big as melons.

"Yes, butt plugs. Does she use the vibrating kind? I'm told they cause a great deal of discomfort. I had a non-vibrating butt plug put in me during a ponygirl scene and it was none too pleasant."

The woman jerked to her feet, spilling a bowl of clam chowder on her black wool skirt. "Who are you?" she demanded, then turned to the group while pointing a shaky finger at me. "This…this *woman*. She's one of those perverts! Help!"

Well, one thing led to another. The short version is that the other members of the group forcibly ushered me to the parking lot, warning me to keep my distance or they'd notify the police. As it turns out, the group was a book club, and they were meeting to discuss Somerset Maugham's classic novel, *Of Human Bondage*.

On the whole, it was a terribly embarrassing moment, made even worse when I encountered the book club to which I belong. They'd just finished their own meeting at the Red Lobster and were headed to their cars when I was unceremoniously tossed out of the restaurant. My costume caused a stir—raised eyebrows, gaping mouths, that sort of thing. Betsy Wigglesdown, chairman of the club, hissed in shock. "I've been hearing stories about your bizarre behavior," she snarled. "We don't want any trollops in the Spinebenders Book Society!" She turned on her heels and stalked away while I gaped in horror.

The message was clear—I wouldn't be welcome at future meetings, which was disappointing, as we were to discuss *Little Women* and I love that book. My drive home that night was long and sad.

Bed and Bondage: If you've ever been to one of the many quaint and homey bed and breakfast inns across the nation, then you have a pretty good idea of what a bed and bondage inn is like. There are, of course, significant differences between the two. Your average bed and breakfast doesn't have a dungeon, nor is there the likelihood of encountering naked people in various forms of bondage sitting across the breakfast table. You will also find that your bed and breakfast hosts are likely to be named Ed and Vicky rather than Lord Ironpole and Lady Whipstick. Also, unless the bed and breakfast owners are Indiana Jones fanatics or just plain crazy, you won't hear the sounds of whips cracking and anguished cries of "Stop! For God's sake stop!"

So, the bed and bondage inn is a bed and breakfast run by kinky people for kinky people. You and your significant other can go to one of these inns and indulge those desires that might not go over well at a Ramada Inn or even a Motel 6. I remember staying in a Motel 6 outside Effingham, Illinois. The couple in the next room made a horrible racket, screaming and shouting all night, punctuated by muffled thuds and breaking glass. I don't know if they were having a scene or merely fighting. The woman kept yelling, "I'll rip your nuts off, you crazy bastard!" Maybe "Crazy Bastard" was the man's kinky title. Hard to tell these days.

Bed and bondage places are surprisingly numerous. There's one in San Francisco called the House of Different Sex Stuff. (It shouldn't come as a surprise that San Francisco has a bed and bondage place. What *is* a surprise is that there is only one.) The House of Different Sex Stuff is run by a maiden woman named Hester, still active in the kinky community as she nears her 90th birthday. While it's nice that Hester retains an energetic lifestyle at her age, some of her patrons do have complaints, such as Hester's use of clear vinyl covers on all the furniture, which tends to stick painfully to the posteriors of those who sit in the parlor and chat while naked. Other gripes involve Hester's frequent and unannounced visits to the dungeon to remind patrons not to make a mess, or her kindhearted but inopportune offers of cookies and milk to those engaged in heavy bondage scenes. Many people have also grumbled that while the house itself is very nice, it has that "old people's smell".

I was able to make telephone contact with the owners of the House of Gloom, a bed and bondage in Michigan operated by a man known as Señor Whip and his wife, Imperial Empress Shirley. Despite his title, Señor Whip does not appear to be Spanish, although he often attempted to speak in a garbled Spanish accent. At least that's what it sounded like.

According to the Imperial Empress Shirley, the house has a large and devoted clientele from all parts of the globe, who brave the harsh Michigan winters to keep the house's four bedrooms occupied near capacity all year long. Such loyalty intrigued me, so I made arrangements to visit the House of Gloom in person.

A week later, I pulled up in front of the house, a one hundred and ten year-old Victorian home of the kind known as a "painted lady." Its exterior color scheme featured a blazing mixture of red, orange and a shade of neon green I've never seen before.

I sat in my car for some time in front of the House of Gloom, wondering if it would be safe for a single woman to enter. After all, I had no idea if any sex fiends lurked inside, ready to pounce at me without warning. Finally, I reminded myself of all the brave ethnographers who had done so much for research, and that was enough to get me out of the car.

A dour man in a tuxedo that appeared to be covered in bloodstains answered my knock on the door. In a deep, monotone voice, he identified himself as Majordomo Ted. Before I could answer, he hissed at me and raised a fist. "What do you want?" he demanded, trembling with anger.

"Nothing," I squeaked in reply.

"Would you like a cup of tea?" he asked, curling his lip.

"Y-yes," I stammered. "That would be nice."

"We don't have any tea!" he roared, trembling even harder.

I shrank back as he bared his teeth and lunged at me. Fortunately, Imperial Empress Shirley rescued me, driving the majordomo away with a sharp stick and a small vial of holy water before ushering me inside.

When I entered the parlor, I expected to see delicate Victorian furnishings. Instead, it was decorated inexplicably in a decor that could only be described as "1970's kitsch". Several beanbag chairs were scattered throughout the room, which was lit only by numerous lava lamps stationed on red plastic milk crates that served as tables. Over the beautiful brick fireplace, a bare black light bulb hanging from the ceiling illuminated a velvet picture of Jimi Hendrix, adding further to the room's mystery. I also noticed the floor was covered with mashed bits of popcorn. In fact, I would discover that every room in the house contained stray piles of popcorn but I was never able to figure out what kinky purpose it might serve.

The gracious Imperial Empress Shirley, dressed for some reason in a Viking costume, including a gigantic horned helmet, led my tour of the facilities. We started with the largest suite, identified by a hand-lettered sign taped to the door as the *Bob Loren Memorial Bedroom*. Mr. Loren, as it turns out, was a visitor some years back who died in that very room when his wife, a dominatrix, accidentally drove thirty-eight roofing nails into his body, resulting in Mr. Loren's very bloody demise.

The furniture in the Loren suite, consisting of an iron bed, battered dresser and a small table, had a familiar appearance. I later learned the reason for this was that it originally came from a Holiday Inn in Paducah, Kentucky, after that facility was remodeled in 1976.

The other bedrooms were similarly eccentric. The furnishings in the *Yogi Berra Bondage Suite* consisted of a stained mattress thrown on the floor and a broken down lawn tractor that leaked oil. The *Deadly Mantis Suite* contained a waterbed, filled some years ago, according to Imperial Empress Shirley, with chocolate pudding. Not only did the room smell like a restaurant dumpster, but the chocolate pudding had congealed to the consistency of concrete, as I painfully discovered when I sat on the bed.

The final guest room, known as the *Cooler Suite,* was furnished with a metal cot with no mattress, a dilapidated toilet and not much else aside from rotting bits of popcorn. Imperial Empress Shirley proudly informed me that the furnishings in the room were obtained when a "torture camp" in an unnamed South American country was overthrown in one of the many revolutions they seem to have down there.

The main feature of any bed and bondage inn is, of course, its dungeon. The facility in the House of Gloom was in a basement room next to a noisy furnace. As we walked down the creaky stairs, my imagination conjured up visions of a dark and gloomy place decorated with sinister bondage equipment, the damp stone walls lined with whips, paddles, restraints and other menacing devices. Instead, the House of Gloom dungeon was a cheery place, well-lit, the walls paneled in walnut and the floor covered by worn but still attractive green shag carpeting. A regulation-sized Ping-Pong table dominated the room, and off to one side, several comfortable recliners faced a widescreen television set. I also noticed a well-used dartboard hanging on a nearby wall.

I should have asked about the non-threatening nature of the dungeon. But now that I think of it, perhaps the proprietors feared a police raid and had disguised their kinky equipment. Certainly, the ping-pong paddles would make fine spanking implements, and maybe there are sadists who enjoy heaving darts at their submissives. And the television, of course, could be used for viewing pornographic videos, though during my visit it was tuned to a marathon of the old *Zorro* TV series.

I felt disappointed that the dungeon didn't seem to have the forbidding atmosphere one would expect in a place of pain and torture. I started to mention this to Imperial Empress Shirley when I was interrupted by the sudden appearance of Señor Whip, uttering a garbled cry as he leapt from behind the furnace. Unlike our previous encounter, in which he was dressed in a plaid shirt and khaki pants, Señor Whip had changed to a t-shirt much too small, with his name crudely lettered across the front in black marker. Unfortunately, the shirt failed to cover his paunch or the bright red thong he wore in place of pants. The rest of his outfit was a blue and green plaid towel pinned around his neck in the manner of a cape.

"I am Señor Whip!" he cried in his feigned Spanish accent, brandishing a short length of rope. "Obey me, or feel my sting!" he added, attempting—and failing—to make the piece of rope crack like a whip.

Imperial Empress Shirley rolled her eyes, then turned her attention to the approach of a stout, balding man dressed in a Girl Scout uniform many sizes too small. "This is one of our house slaves," she explained to me.

The man held a covered silver platter in his hands. He thrust it toward Imperial Empress Shirley and spoke in a quiet voice. "It's time, Mistress."

Imperial Empress Shirley's eyes blazed with anticipation as Señor Whip stood by her side. "Uncover the plate," she said in an emotional voice.

The house slave lifted the cover, revealing a large stack of waffles.

"Say it!" demanded Señor Whip. "Say it, damn you!"

"Yes, Master," said the slave. He cleared his throat and spoke in a high falsetto. "It's waffle time!"

Like starving animals, my hosts dove for the plate, knocking the waffles all over the dungeon floor. I had to duck the sharp horns on Imperial Empress Shirley's Viking headgear as she and her husband scrambled after the food, stuffing their faces and uttering growls.

After a few minutes, all of the waffles had been consumed, leaving only a few scattered crumbs on the carpet. Señor Whip scuttled back behind the furnace and Imperial Empress Shirley replaced her Viking hat and escorted me upstairs as though nothing had happened.

I felt I had seen enough of the House of Gloom at this point and turned to say goodbye to Imperial Empress Shirley. She had quietly disappeared, however, and I found myself facing Majordomo Ted again. "Her Imperial Empress has been detained," he said in a mournful voice. "Allow me to show you out." He then jabbed a dirty finger in the general direction of the front door.

Feeling ill at ease in the presence of this man, I hurried to the relative safely of the front porch. "Next time, close the door, you hideous fool!" Majordomo Ted hissed, slamming the door much harder than necessary.

As I drove away, I heard the muffled yells of Señor Whip wafting up from the basement, along with the sound of broken glass coming from elsewhere in the house. I thanked my lucky stars that I was not prone to kinkiness and would never have to visit this place again.

Chapter Eight

Techniques—It's not as easy as it looks, that's for sure

THE CRAFT OF KINK

It's true that virtually anyone can get a hold of a paddle or a set of restraints and dive in the kinky pool. That doesn't mean, however, that one would be good at it. During my research, I saw many people whose expertise with various kinky implements was truly impressive.

I remember, in particular, a domme in a bondage club wielding floggers in both hands as she battered the buttocks of her slave bent over a table. With just a flick of her wrists, the floggers swished through the air in perfect timing, one strike after another. The tails of the floggers separated as she swung, making them resemble fans in the hands of an expert geisha. I watched, fascinated, until her slave suddenly jumped up from the table and ran away, knocking over a row of leather slaves standing at attention while a dom dressed as a Roman general yelled orders at them. The leather men fell like dominoes as the slave crashed through them, clutching at his reddened, striped behind.

I also recall a bondage scene where a dom utilized Japanese rope bondage to weave a dress around his sub. I couldn't imagine the amount of work that went into perfecting such exquisite artistry! As the sub squirmed in her tight bondage, the dom attached a wire to the rope dress and hoisted the sub a good ten feet above our heads, where she stretched out above us like a magician's assistant floating in air.

"Watch this," the dom said, giving the sub a push. She spun, faster and faster, until she was a blur. Then the wire broke and she went shooting off to the far end of the room, landing on a woman giving a demonstration of play piercing. The slave being used as a pincushion was pierced in a way the woman hadn't intended, as the needle shot through his nose and into one ear.

As my research went on, I learned to respect the kinky artists who had put in so much work perfecting their craft. I knew I could never approach their level of expertise, but after reading Uncle Henry's library and then going into the field to experience kinky behavior firsthand, I felt ready to initiate my own scenes and develop my kinky technique. After all, as the philosopher said, there is no experience like experience. No, I don't know which philosopher it was. There are a lot of them, so I'm sure at one point or another one of them said something about experience. I'm not going to worry about it.

Leaving philosophy aside, the important point is that as an ethnographer, I needed as much real world experience as I could get on my own terms. And so the next phase of my research began, although things didn't go exactly as I planned.

MY LIFE AS A DOMME

I decided my participation would consist of becoming a professional dominatrix, at least temporarily. I had been posing as Mistress Dominique from time to time, but mainly in the course of interviewing my subjects. The time had come to transform myself into a domme in both word and deed. It turned out to be a rather expensive proposition. I knew I needed suitable attire to inflict fear and whatnot in my slaves, but my earlier efforts in this direction were less than successful, as people either giggled or gawked in horror. Reluctantly, I decided to get professional advice, but since my town doesn't have a fetish clothing store, I was forced to go to a costume shop.

The salesclerk at Kim's Kostumes greeted my request for a dominatrix outfit with a puzzled stare. When I explained what I wanted, she grabbed a plastic sword lying on a counter and glared at me like she feared an imminent attack. It took a while, but I finally convinced her I wasn't a fiend, and she agreed to show me a representative sample of the store's wares.

I had no interest in the bee costume, though the long plastic stinger mounted on the posterior might have been useful as a torture toy. Neither did I care for the squid outfit. How could I handle an unruly slave with all those tentacles flopping around? The harem costume tempted me, being rather exotic, but it looked too fragile to handle the kind of activity I expected to experience in my new persona.

An hour later, the pile of rejected costumes had grown large, as had my feeling of discouragement. Then the clerk brought out a fairy princess costume, gleaming white with silver sparkles dusted over it. Yes! This was the uniform I needed to inspire servitude and submission! The flounced skirt was daring, being on the short side, but the beautiful white petticoats would serve to keep prying eyes at bay. Mysterious, powerful, awe-inspiring—that's what the costume represented.

The accessories made the costume even more fearsome. The tiara covered in faux diamonds was elegantly regal, and the silver magic wand with a glittery star at the tip would serve me well. I envisioned myself waving it in a menacing fashion as I barked out commands to the cowering masses. Best of all were the translucent fairy wings attached to the back of the dress. The dominatrix as evil fairy! That would be my role. Well, Mistress Dominique's role, anyway.

As I twirled in front of a mirror in my new outfit, scattering sparkles on the floor, my only regret was that the fairy gown didn't come in an evil shade of black. That would have made for a more formidable look but I decided that was a minor problem and easily overcome by utilizing my forceful personality.

Next, I needed appropriate equipment to use on my slaves-to-be, so I stopped by Higgins Hardware. I puzzled for a moment when the clerk, a neatly groomed young man, greeted me as though we had met before. Finally, realization hit. Even though his nametag identified him as "Stewart," he was actually Lucifer Nightshade Hell, the Goth I'd interviewed earlier. He didn't look particularly Gothy that day in the store, wearing a bright plaid shirt and pressed slacks, his blond hair short and well groomed. Perhaps he had switched kinks and become a teenist.

After my initial reception at the costume shop, I felt too embarrassed to tell Stewart what I was after, so I wandered the aisles picking up whatever items I thought would be useful. I ended up purchasing a toilet plunger, a large mallet, a posthole digger, one of those big bicycle locks, twenty feet of towing chain, some garden tools, a flyswatter, a screen door and some furniture polish. (The furniture polish wasn't part of my kinky equipment. Higgins Hardware had a sale on Pledge, so I stocked up.)

Stewart didn't seem to think twice about my purchases, chatting amiably with me as he rang up my purchases. I learned he had decided to experiment with a uniform kink similar to Emily, Queen of Bonerland. At least that's what it sounded like. He said he had become a drag queen, so I assumed he liked dressing up in a velvet robe and a crown.

After leaving the hardware store, I stopped at Vic's Price Gougers for extra rolls of paper towels, on the assumption that the dominatrix business was likely to be fairly messy. I also grabbed a large jar of hot peppers in case I met anyone into sploshing. They were cheap because the expiration date had passed but I certainly wasn't going to eat the nasty things.

Having secured my dominatrix uniform and proper tools, I headed to the offices of the local newspaper and placed the following advertisement in the "Personals" section of the classifieds:

YOU VILE WORM! *I am Mistress Dominique and I order you to serve me NOW! Once you enter my dungeon of distress you will be made to feel very uncomfortable as I torture your body and mind in ways that would make your poor mother sick to her stomach if she only knew what kind of twisted activities you were up to when her back was turned. Call me at 555-4477 and prepare for your journey into uneasiness and trepidation!*

The man at the classifieds counter looked at me like I was from outer space when he read my advertisement. He took it into a back room and a few moments later I heard uproarious laughter. No doubt it was a nervous reaction at the thought of an actual dominatrix standing in their offices. When he returned to the counter, he made odd sounds that almost sounded like giggling, and had to stop at one point and wipe away a tear or two. I felt empowered at the effect I had on the poor man. Perhaps I was naturally dominant and didn't know it!

My advertisement appeared in the paper the next morning. I eagerly organized my costume and equipment and waited for my future slaves to call. Unfortunately, the telephone remained steadfastly silent all that day and for the next week.

Well, that's not completely true. I received numerous calls from telemarketers that made me wish I could track them down and beat them senseless. I also heard from my mother, who was quite vociferous in her disapproval of my activities of late. "First we find out that Henry is a raging pervert and now I hear stories that you're running around in weird outfits and hanging out at every strip club in town!" Mother howled. "I tried to bring you up right and this is how you repay me!" She had much more to say, but it was all along the same lines, so you get the idea. Oh, and I did get a call from Aunt Ruth, who went into great detail about her new boyfriend, Octavio. Not once did she mention Uncle Henry. Still in denial, poor woman.

As nervous as I felt at the thought of dominating a man, I found myself acutely disappointed at the lack of response. I was ready to give up on this particular experiment when I received the following call:

Mistress Dominique: Hello?

Caller: (muffled sounds of heavy breathing)

MD: Hello? Is anyone there?

Caller: (sounds of breathing become louder)

MD: I don't have time for this. If you don't say something I'm going to hang up.

Caller: What are you wearing?

MD: What? Who is this?

Caller: I'll bet you don't wear panties, do you?

MD: Of all the nerve! What do you want?

Caller: You know what I'd like to do? I'd like to cover you with whipped cream and lick it all off, real slow like. Yeah, that would be nice.

MD: What on earth are you babbling about? Are you sure you have the right number?

Caller: Oh yeah, I got your number all right. Bet you'd look good with a cherry and some chocolate syrup to go with that whipped cream.

MD: Tom Bentlemeyer, is that you? Have you been drinking again?

Caller: No, I'm not that guy. My name is Richard, but you can call me Dick. Heh, heh, Dick. Get it?

MD: Well, Dick, what do you want?

Caller: Oh God, you said "Dick". Oh God.

MD: Look, Dick, I'm very busy. Either tell me what you want or I'm hanging up.

Caller: (sounds of moaning) You said "Dick" again! I'm coming! I'm coming!

MD: You are most certainly not coming here until you state your business!

Caller: You said "coming!" Aaaaahhhhh!

MD: If you're sick you should go to the hospital. Hello? Hello?

Caller: Oh God, that was great! See ya!

MD: What was great? Nothing happened. Hello? He must have hung up. How rude.

I later recounted this episode to a dominatrix acquaintance and learned I had experienced **phone sex** for the first time. Of course, I had heard of the phone sex phenomenon before, having seen all the advertisements from lonely nymphomaniacs in the back of our local alternative newspaper, but I have to say it wasn't nearly as wonderful as it's made out to be. In fact, it did nothing for me at all.

Nevertheless, I chalked it up to experience and pressed on with my research.

My acquaintance also chided me for not getting a credit card number at the onset of the call. I must confess it never occurred to me. Afterward, I tried to get in the habit of asking all my callers for a credit card number but that proved to be a bit of a sticky issue with my friends, especially the woman from the Harold Leipnitz Film Appreciation Society, who called me a "disgusting prostitute" and hung up. I fear they will never readmit me into their midst. Oh well.

After several weeks and only the one call from Dick, I determined that my newspaper advertisement was lacking in some way, so I headed back to the newspaper to insert a new advertisement, reproduced below:

YOU SCUMBALL! *Enter my garden of unearthly delights, you weed! Let me take control of your mind and body with my garden tools and other instruments of hideously fiendish torture! I am Mistress Dominique! Worship my shoes and other personal garments, some of which are slightly odoriferous, and I will reward you with a severe thrashing of some sort! I order you to call me now at 555-4477!*

Once again, the man who took my order at the classifieds counter went though the same paroxysm of fear that manifested itself in uncontrolled laughter. This time, several of his colleagues came over to look at me and they too had the same hysterical reaction. I felt sorry for them, using false bravado to conceal their dark dreams of cowering before my female superiority.

The next morning I crossed my fingers and hoped for the best as I once again prepared myself and the equipment. Happily, the new advertisement resulted in a response that afternoon, from a man identifying himself as "slave Eddie," who wanted to come to my home for a session of professional domination. We negotiated a fee, though slave Eddie seemed surprised at my demand for $15.00, making me worry for a moment that I might be charging too much. With that settled, I gave him instructions on what to wear and said I would expect him on my doorstep at precisely 2:00 p.m. the next day.

I arose bright and early so I'd have plenty of time to prepare for slave Eddie's visit. Normally, I don't wear a great deal of makeup, mostly a little lipstick and mascara, but all the dominatrixes I'd seen on the Internet caked it on fairly heavily, so I did the same. I must say, it was shocking to see the finished product in the bathroom mirror. Thick blue eye shadow, flaming red lipstick, both contrasting nicely with the sparkly white fairy princess costume. Once I got my tiara in place and practiced brandishing my magic wand, I knew any man who looked at me would be unable to resist the temptation to fall to his knees and beg to be in my service.

Now that I looked the part, I double-checked the equipment in my "dungeon". Actually, it was the basement, but it was dark and smelt a little of dampness, so I thought it would provide a suitable environment for the evil about to take place. I put my selection of "play toys" from the hardware store on a card table next to the pile of boxes containing the reading material I'd brought over from Uncle Henry's den. I decided to tie my client to the water pipes running across the ceiling of the basement, so I looped a couple of lengths of rope over the pipes and got them ready. All I needed was for my client to arrive.

The doorbell rang at 1:58 p.m. He's early, I thought to myself. I already have a good excuse to inflict punishment on him. I strode confidently to the door and jerked it open, brandishing the magic wand fiercely. "You're early, you worm!" I shouted in my meanest voice. "You will pay for this!" Then I noticed my visitor wasn't slave Eddie, but Margaret Beemsterboer from the Savvy Seeders garden club.

The color drained from her face as she took in my makeup and fairy princess costume. "Don't hit me!" she screamed, her eyes wide as she pointed at the magic wand I still held over my head. I quickly started to explain what I was doing, dressed as I was, but Margaret fled down the front steps to her car. She fumbled in her purse for her keys, glancing at me every few seconds. Finally, she found the keys and hurled herself in the car.

Events went downhill at that point. Margaret's car roared to life, but in her panic, she didn't pay attention backing out of my driveway, and thus didn't see slave Eddie pulling in. Their cars smacked together with a horrible crunch. My client, a chubby, balding man, jumped out of his car to see how much damage was done, an unwise decision on his part, since I had instructed him to arrive dressed only in a black leather G-string, matching collar and nipple clamps. When Eddie tapped on Margaret's window to get her attention, she began screaming uncontrollably and hopping in her seat like it was on fire.

I knew I had to do something to get this unfortunate situation under control, so I ran to Margaret's car, hoping to shoo slave Eddie away so Margaret could leave. My slave's mouth dropped when he saw my costume. "What the fuck?" he mumbled. He turned to leave but tripped and fell next to Margaret's vehicle. This set Margaret off even more and she pounded on the horn while screaming for the police.

As luck—all bad, it would seem—would have it, a patrol car was in the area and stopped to see what the commotion was about. Still on the ground, slave Eddie became agitated at the arrival of the police and decided to hide under Margaret's car. Unfortunately, he managed to get the chain connecting his nipple clamps caught on the bottom edge of the vehicle and began thrashing his legs wildly. Feeling the car move, Margaret turned pale, holding her head with both hands while rocking back and forth in the front seat, shrieking at irregular intervals. My slave added to the cacophony, howling in pain as he frantically attempted to disentangle himself.

A policeman strolled up the driveway and looked at slave Eddie, still writhing on the ground, then gave me a hard stare. Finally, he noticed Margaret, still rocking back and forth and crying hysterically. Shaking his head, he nudged Eddie with his boot. "Leave the woman alone, you rotten little pervert. I told you to knock this crap off in public. Now get out of here!"

Poor Eddie got up so fast that he ripped the nipple clamps off his body. He fled to his car sobbing in pain, leaving the clamps dangling from Margaret's vehicle. As Eddie sped away, the policeman turned his attention to me. "Well, well, what are you supposed to be, a perverted fairy godmother? You wouldn't happen to be running a whorehouse for bad little boys like Eddie, would you?"

I started to explain the situation when Margaret flung open her door, catching the officer in the small of the back. He fell on top of me, the impact causing me to accidentally whack him on the head with my magic wand. I didn't think I'd hit him that hard but he lost consciousness and I found myself sprawled on the ground underneath a heavy policeman. As I struggled to free myself, Margaret began a strange dance in the driveway. Drool ran from one corner of her mouth as she waved her arms in the air and screeched incoherently.

At that point, my next-door neighbor, Pastor Herman from the First United Presbyterian church, ran into my yard to see what the ruckus was about. "I'm saved!" Margaret howled. She made a beeline for him, shrieking and waving her arms. Pastor Herman is a man of slight build and tried to evade Margaret's advance but with no success. He collapsed when she tried to leap into his arms. Still trapped under the policeman, I watched in shock as Margaret sat on Pastor Herman's chest, tearing at his shirt and babbling while the poor man gasped for breath.

A second police car arrived and two officers jumped out, guns drawn. I must admit the situation appeared peculiar. I was still attempting to evacuate myself from underneath the unconscious officer and Margaret looked like she was trying to strangle Pastor Herman. One of the officers yelled into his walkie-talkie about "backup," then pointed his gun at me and told me to drop the wand. The other officer shouted orders to Margaret, who didn't seem to hear him in her frenzy, so he shot her in the face with pepper spray, which finally got her off of Pastor Herman but made her howl even louder as she clawed at her eyes.

I believe a total of ten police cars eventually made their way to my home. A dozen officers ran through the yard chasing Margaret, who waved a piece of Pastor Herman's shirt like a flag. They finally cornered her in the shrubbery and subdued her with the aid of a Taser. She was barely conscious when they handcuffed her and threw her in the back of a police van.

They revived the unfortunate officer who collided with my magic wand and put him on a stretcher, which was then loaded into one of the ambulances that had arrived. Then I was handcuffed, the first time I experienced the cold feel of the restraints. I can't say I enjoyed it. In fact, it was one of the least erotic experiences I've ever had! After the cuffing, the officers shoved me in the police van. Margaret cringed in the corner and spit at me, but then her eyes rolled back in her head and she was quiet.

Eventually, the whole situation was resolved and no charges were filed, although it was difficult to convince the police that my beaning of the officer with the magic wand was accidental. I felt terribly embarrassed explaining my costume, as well as the reason for slave Eddie's arrival at my home, although my story provoked a great deal of hilarity amongst the officers. Poor Margaret was taken to the mental health ward of the local hospital and remained there for quite some time. Pastor Herman resigned his ministry and moved out of town shortly afterward. No one seems to know his whereabouts.

DOMME TRAINEE

It shouldn't come as a surprise that I became disheartened by the disastrous outcome of my initial foray into domination. For a time I contemplated giving up on this project altogether but with the passage of time, my spirit revived and I was determined to tackle the dominatrix experience via an alternative route. Happily, an opportunity came my way when I began communicating in a chat room—KJ's Parlor of Pillage, I think it was called—with a professional dominatrix, Lady PaperCut. I was immediately taken by her non-de-plume and I still think it's the best I've encountered. I *hate* paper cuts! Imagine a submissive, trembling in fear at the thought of a vicious domme waving a sharp piece of paper. You can't do much better than that!

After we got to know one another, I explained the nature of my research. My enthusiasm must have been infectious, as she soon offered to take me on as her assistant and tutor me in the ways of professional domination.

As luck would have it, Lady PaperCut lived in a nearby city, so I packed my fairy princess domination outfit, minus the magic wand, which the police confiscated. They declared it to be a "deadly weapon," although they snickered as they did so. It was badly bent anyway, so it wasn't of much use.

Once packed, I headed for Lady PaperCut's home, which also served as her dungeon. An hour later, I arrived at the designated address, located in a desolate, windswept area at the foot of a large hill. My heart sank when I realized the Palace of Torture was in a trailer park. Lady PaperCut's posts had given me the impression of a large estate, surrounded by gardens lovingly tended by willing slaves who were regularly tortured in a cavernous dungeon. Obviously, this was not to be the case.

My knock upon the dented aluminum door was answered by a rotund woman with a beefy face punctuated by a broad, red nose. She wore a shapeless housedress in a faded floral print, her reddish hair mixed with gray peaking from a red banana covering her head. A frown split her face when she saw the small suitcase containing my dominatrix equipment. "Whatever you're selling, we don't want none of that shit 'round here!" she yelled, slamming the door in my face.

Obviously, she had misconstrued my purpose, so I knocked again. This time she didn't bother to open the door but merely yelled something about setting the dogs on me if I didn't get my "spotty ass" away from her home. I turned away, at a loss of what to do. As I pondered the situation, a cloud passed in front of the sun, darkening the area, and I noticed the other denizens of the trailer park scurrying furtively, as though some great evil had descended on them.

I decided to make one more effort to gain admittance and called out as loudly as I could that I was her friend from the chat list and had come for my dominatrix training. I shouldn't have yelled that last bit, as it seemed to make the trailer park people even more nervous. Faces appeared in windows, gawking in my direction before the curtains were snapped shut. To make matters worse, a thunderstorm began to form over the hill rising above the trailer park, letting loose an ominous rumble as the wind picked up.

After what seemed like an eternity, Lady PaperCut opened the door and ushered me inside, apologizing for the misunderstanding. "Shit fire!" she exclaimed. "I thought you were one of them encyclopedia salesmen! Those bastards come around here all the fuckin' time!"

I stood in what appeared to be her living room, although it was hard to tell, as most of the furniture was covered with hundreds of old *TV Guide* magazines. Also to be found in great abundance were cats. Some sprawled on their backs, asleep, while others played amidst the towering stacks of magazines. I lost count at twenty-five felines, and from the screeching emanating from elsewhere in the trailer, there were likely many more.

"I gotta get my fucking slaves in here to do a little cleanin' up," Lady PaperCut muttered as she brushed away a cat attempting to crawl up her leg. "I've had ol' Leroy up on the roof putting on some new tar and the rest of 'em have been makin' me a little vegetable garden out back, but we ain't done much with the interior décor." Kicking at a pair of cats busily mating at her feet, Lady PaperCut led me to the kitchen and pointed at a rickety stool. "Take the weight off, hon, and I'll crack open a couple of brewskis."

I sat gingerly on the stool and watched as my host pulled two cans of beer from a battered and stained refrigerator. "Too bad Mickey ain't here," she said, her smile revealing the loss of several teeth. "You should see what he can do with an empty beer can. Smacks it right upside his forehead!" She demonstrated with an imaginary can. "Smashes those suckers down to nothin'!"

I had no idea what she was talking about, so I feigned an approving smile as she plopped a real can in front of me. I'm not a drinker but I wanted to be sociable, so I took a small sip. As I feared, the beer tasted horrible but I managed not to choke.

"Suck down your suds and I'll take you out back to the dungeon," Lady PaperCut grinned. She pointed out the kitchen window to a small wooden shed, listing slightly to one side, its tarpaper roof flapping in the wind. "It's out there yonder."

So much for my visions of working in a state-of-the-art dungeon. For a moment, I thought about going home but I decided to see things through, since it might be a long time before another dominatrix offered to train me in her dark art. With an effort, I managed to finish the horrid brew—I noticed it was called Blitz 45 for no apparent reason and made a mental note to write the manufacturer a letter complaining about the taste of their product. Almost immediately, I began to feel somewhat lightheaded, not an altogether unpleasant sensation.

Lady PaperCut picked up my valise and led me to the shed/dungeon. "You picked a good day to come, dearie," she smirked. "I got an appointment with Crazy Morty this evening. Oh, he's a real shitkicker, he is!"

Shooing cats from our path, my host led me to the shed but had trouble getting the door open. "Goddamn thing is swollen from the rain last night," she grunted. "I told that lazy son of a bitch Larry to fix this door but he forgot. That boy is gonna get his ass tanned big time!" She stared at the door with venomous eyes and gave the handle a mighty pull. With a cracking sound she wrenched the door from its hinges, watching as it fell to the ground. "Yep, that boy is gettin' his ass whacked good," she mumbled as we entered her lair.

I had hopes the inside might be more impressive than the outside but it was not to be. The shed had a dirt floor, which seemed to me to be highly unsanitary. A solitary light bulb hanging from the ceiling by a wire was the only source of light, barely illuminating a rough wooden table about six feet long. I noticed worn and cracked leather straps attached to each corner.

"Welcome to the Palace of Torture," Lady PaperCut said, giving me a slap on the back. "Hell, I know it don't look like much, but it gets the job done."

I attempted a smile, not knowing what to say.

She pointed at my valise. "I gotta find the cattle prod. Go ahead and get your sex duds on."

In the dim light, I hurriedly unpacked my dominatrix attire and dressed. I was adjusting the tiara on my head when I heard footsteps, followed by the appearance of a figure in the doorway. I gaped at a broad shouldered man nearly seven feet tall, wearing bib overalls with no shirt, allowing me a look at his heavily muscled arms. He held a long white rod with a thick red handle at one end and what appeared to be an electrical plug at the other. Spitting a wad of brown goo to the side, he grinned and tugged at the bill of a soiled yellow baseball cap advertising seed corn.

"Lady P. said she had a new girl workin' with her," he rumbled. "That's you, huh? You sure are pretty, all dressed up like a fairy and all."

I nodded, too intimidated by the man's sheer bulk to say anything.

He thrust a massive paw at me. "I'm Crazy Morty. They call me that 'cause I fell off the top of a grain elevator once. They said I went around talkin' French for a month afore I got my wits back." He stopped and spit again. "Leastwise, they think it was French, but I don't know no French. Maybe it was German, 'cept I don't know none of that, neither."

I felt the muscles in the back of my neck tighten. "I see," I squeaked. "And…and you are here for a domination session?"

"Yep." He removed his hat, revealing a head flatter than anything I'd ever seen. It was hard to take my eyes from that skull but I managed it after a few moments.

"Well." I toyed will the hem of my fairy skirt. "As soon as Lady PaperCut returns, we'll get started, okay?"

He shoved the long white rod at me. "I seen Lady P. outside and she gave me the cattle prod. Said for you to go ahead 'cause one of the cats is throwin' up hairballs on the stove and she's got to tend to that."

My stomach clenched as I took the implement. "I see. That's, um, unfortunate. About the cats, I mean."

"Hate cats myself, but Lady P. is crazy 'bout 'em." He unbuttoned his overalls and let them drop to the floor, leaving him dressed in stained white underpants and thick-soled work boots. "Guess I'm ready," he said, smiling.

"Ah. It would appear that way, wouldn't it?" I said, trying to coax some moisture into my mouth. My brain whirled as I tried to think of what to do next.

"Lady P. usually straps me to the table," Morty said helpfully.

I nodded. "Certainly. We'll start with the table."

Morty covered the shed in three giant strides and sprawled on the table, causing it to groan ominously. "Now you got to strap me in."

With nervous fingers, I tightened the leather around Morty's thick wrists and ankles. "How's that? Are you comfortable?"

He nodded, shaking the table. "You bet. Lady P. would start torturin' me with the prod now. If I start talkin' French or German again, don't worry none about it. I'll be right as rain pretty soon after."

I gripped the cattle prod and felt a button on the handle. This was my first real experience with electrical play and I wasn't sure what to do. One vital bit of information I lacked was that one should never use any kind of electric implement above the shoulders, as it can cause permanent harm. If I had only known this, my experience with Morty might have been more successful.

"Start in anytime you want," said Morty. He wrinkled his nose as a gnat landed on it, then scratched it with his right hand, shredding the restraint in the process. "Aw, dang! Lady P. is gonna be madder than hell at me for breakin' her bondage table again."

I gawked for a moment then managed to find words. "Well, we can pretend your right arm is in bondage, okay?"

"You're the boss," Morty said, his dark eyes fixed on mine.

I took a deep breath and regarded the cattle prod. It wasn't in my nature to deliberately hurt someone, and yet, as a professional dominatrix, that was a large part of my duties. Finally, I pointed the prod at Morty, closed my eyes and pushed the button.

I should have kept my eyes open. The prod landed on Morty's neck and when I activated the device, a jolt of electricity shot into his head.

"Arrrrrrgh!" Morty screamed in agony. I screamed in terror as he got up from the table, snapping the remaining leather straps like tissue paper. "Mes ébullitions de cerveau comme la viande! Mes globes oculaires sont sur le feu!" he screamed, swinging his arms wildly around the shed. A rumble erupted from his throat, so low it made my teeth vibrate. Bumping against the bondage table, he raised a huge fist and brought it down, turning the table into kindling.

Lady PaperCut appeared at the door, holding a vomiting cat. She gaped at the scene inside. "Holy shit! What the hell did you do to him?"

Morty turned on her and snarled. She squeaked and disappeared before I could answer her question. I ducked as Morty stumbled past me and brushed against a wall, causing the shed to tremble. Tripping over my valise, he banged his head against the light bulb hanging from the ceiling. It exploded in a shower of sparks, igniting a mound of hay piled in a corner. Fire erupted immediately.

"Le mauvais du feu! Doit détruire le feu!" With a thundering crash, Morty smashed a hole in a wall and walked stiff-legged toward the nearby hill. He hadn't climbed far when a bolt of lightening struck him on the head. With smoke drifting from his hair and shoes, he continued on as though nothing happened.

I've often heard submissives talk about **endorphins**, chemicals released by the body in response to pain. Apparently, receiving a sound beating causes the release of so many endorphins that the sub experiences a high not unlike that from consuming illegal narcotics. I believe the sheer terror I felt in the shed caused a similar reaction in me. As if in a daze, I ran to my car and scrabbled to unlock the door in the growing gloom of the evening. Once inside, I looked at the shed, completely consumed by flames. The wind began gusting violently as screams pierced the rumbling of the growing thunderstorm. I heard a shotgun blast and then another. The whole trailer park sprang to life as people ran past me, holding pitchforks and torches.

An elderly man dressed in what appeared to be lederhosen stuck his face up to the car window. "Kill the monster!" he yelled, brandishing a wooden club before running off to join the mob pursuing Morty.

I punched the accelerator, wishing I had picked a car with more power than fuel efficiency. I managed to steer out of the trailer park but my hands shook so badly I had to stop a half-mile later at a scenic overlook. Dusk had settled, but I could see a plume of white smoke rising from the trailer park. Behind it, the flames from dozens of torches weaved through the trees like angry fireflies as the trailer park people raced toward the top of the hill. A flash of lightning lit up the area, allowing me to see Morty silhouetted on the hill's peak, clutching his head. Perhaps it was the storm, but I swore I heard a thundering growl.

When Morty started grabbing boulders and hurling them at his pursuers, I knew it was time to leave. I made it home in one piece and immediately locked the doors and pulled the curtains closed. As I stood shaking in the kitchen, I remembered a bottle of wine Aunt Ruth had brought me as a souvenir of her trip to Italy. With shaking hands, I pulled it from its perch behind a squash in the back of the refrigerator and poured myself a glass. It didn't taste very good, but I felt a warm glow in my stomach and my hands weren't shaking as much. I thought another glass wouldn't hurt, and it didn't. Neither did a third or a fourth.

I can't remember when I went to sleep that night. I awoke on the kitchen floor, the empty wine bottle at my side. Under that was my "Things to Do" notepad. The scrawl on the top page didn't look like my handwriting, but apparently I'd given myself one chore for the day: find out who invented ethnography and strangle them.

Chapter Nine

Advice from Mistress Dominique

MAKE YOUR DUNGEON A HAPPIER PLACE!

After all the work I put into creating an effective kinky moniker, you can imagine my surprise when I discovered *another* Mistress Dominique living nearby. It was disappointing, of course, to realize that my kinky identity wasn't unique but we live in a strange and mysterious world where coincidence sometimes intrudes on our orderly lives.

The other Mistress Dominique is a lifestyle dominatrix and Avon representative. She lives in Shumway, Illinois, with her submissive husband, Artie, plus six cats, a horse and a man named Rainbow who sleeps in their storage shed. They aren't sure why Rainbow is there, but he keeps the shed clean so they don't much care.

I was fortunate enough to meet Mistress Dominique when I ran out of foot care crème and decided to see if Avon had anything that could keep my heels from getting so cracked and rough. Turns out they did, and one afternoon I answered the doorbell to find Mistress Dominique on the doorstep holding a little Avon bag.

It was lucky she had that bag, as I might not have let her in otherwise. I was greeted with the sight of a tall woman with dramatic makeup, her black hair pulled back in a severe bun. But what really caught my eye was that she was clad nearly head to toe in black patent leather, not a look you normally expect from an Avon representative. Even so, when

I saw the bag clutched in her leather-gloved hand, I knew relief for my feet was at hand and happily let her in.

As I wrote out a check for my purchase, we started chatting and I couldn't help but make a small comment about her rather unconventional attire. That was when she told me about her life as a dominatrix and how she always dressed in leather. She went on to tell me the Avon people were none too happy about her personal presentation but since she had the highest number of sales in our area, they didn't complain too much. Spying the coiled whip attached to her belt, I understood why this might be true. It's hard to turn down any salesperson who might use such a frightening implement if an unfortunate customer didn't buy enough wrinkle cream or lip liner.

It occurred to me that the other Mistress Dominique might be of great help to my project, so I told her of my research into all things kinky. Happily, she agreed to come aboard as an adviser to those with questions of a kinky nature and within a few days we had made our project known to various kinky Internet lists with which Mistress Dominique was familiar. She was immediately inundated with questions from confused kinksters, some of which are reproduced in this chapter. Hopefully these questions are broad enough that they will help you, dear reader, in answering some of your concerns as well.

Dear Mistress Dominique,

My husband, Edward, recently said that he wanted something new in our relationship. It's been slow for us in the bedroom, if you know what I mean, so I was all for anything that might put the spark back in our lovemaking. Unfortunately, my husband's idea of something new involved balloons. Balloons! What kind of weirdness is that?

He must have gotten the idea from one of those porno places on the Internet.

I told Edward I was willing to try anything once, but I had no idea things would turn out so horribly. I expected him to bring in some party balloons, maybe filled with helium but instead he brought in a huge bundle of rubber and a metal canister of compressed air. He hooked up the canister to the bundle and started blowing it up. It turned out to be a weather balloon!

It quickly filled the bedroom. I yelled for Edward to stop but he was on the other side of the balloon and couldn't hear me. Finally, it got so big it threatened to crush me against the bedroom wall. I panicked and managed to crawl under the bed, yelling all the while, but Eddie started moaning and couldn't hear me. In the meantime, the balloon grew bigger and bigger.

I don't know what happened next. I heard a huge BOOM! It felt like the whole house had blown up. The bed and I ended up in a heap in a corner and when I crawled out from underneath, the bedroom was devastated, with bits of rubber stuff all over, the furniture smashed and the air full of feathers from our pillows. One wall had a giant hole in it and all the windows were blown out.

Worst of all, there was no sign of my husband. I had the police come over and they looked everywhere but couldn't find him. I didn't want to tell them what happened, but eventually I had to give them the whole story. Some of the police officers laughed. Others gave me the skunk eye, like I was making the whole thing up.

It's been two weeks now and my husband is still missing. Our neighbor down the street found one of Edward's shoes clogging his gutters. Another neighbor three blocks over found a pair of Edward's pants in a tree.

I miss Eddie so much. Why won't he come home? I don't know how to deal with all this loneliness.

All by Myself

Dear All by Myself,

I don't suppose you had a video camera running at the time, did you? That would have been a hoot to watch!

SINcerely,

Mistress Dominique

Dear Mistress Dominique,

My wife and I often engage in kinky activities and enjoy ourselves very much. She's into S&M a little, so once in a while I tie her to the bed and whip her lightly. Lately she said this wasn't enough and she wanted to be punished with something called a "frogger". At least that's what it sounded like—she's Australian and has a thick accent. I couldn't find a frogger in any our of sex toy catalogs, so I did the next best thing and tied a frog to the end of my whip. Problem is, she hated being hit with the frogger. It made a terrible mess after a few strokes and the frog began screeching, which made my wife cry. Did I do something wrong here? Perhaps my whip technique needs work or maybe I need to attach more frogs to the whip.

Perplexed in Muncie

Dear Perplexed,

Do you and your wife have any children? Please tell me you don't.

SINcerely,

Mistress Dominique

Dear Mistress Dominique,

I recently became involved with a man who introduced me to the kinky lifestyle but there are many things I don't understand. I hope you can help. My boyfriend says what really turns him on is his "beer suit". It's just what it sounds like, a whole suit he made out of old Blatz beer cans. It smells horrible because I don't think he cleaned the cans out first, but that's not the real problem.

What I don't get is that after we go to the trouble of getting him into the suit, he lights a couple of those Fourth of July sparklers and runs into the street. He just stands there blocking traffic and singing the Canadian national anthem until one of the neighbors calls the police. Later he calls from jail and says I have to bail him out. Like an idiot, I always do, and when we get home he says it was the best sex he ever had and goes to sleep, still wearing that stupid beer can suit. I don't know what sex he's talking about because he never touches me. He seems so happy but I'm not getting much out of it. I know it's my fault because I don't know anything about kinky sex. Can you help?

Confused Newbie

Dear Confused Newbie,

The next time lover boy decides to dress up like the Tin Man on a bender, don't wait until a neighbor calls the cops. Call the local recycling folks and have them collect your boyfriend. Oh, he'll probably end up being put in a furnace and melted down into slag but that will give you a chance to find a new guy. Look for someone who is into more normal kinky pursuits like drinking your urine while dressed as a German naval officer or a man who enjoys being hit with a garden trowel during sex.

SINcerely,

Mistress Dominique

Dear Mistress Dominique,

I keep running into people at munches and play parties who say they are "Old Guard". They get this snotty look and act like they expect me to throw myself on the ground at their feet. What's up with that?

Mr. Cheese

Dear Mr. Cheese,

The Old Guard is a group of people who started the BDSM community many, many years ago. Now they've reached their senior years and their behavior tends to get erratic at times. It's doubtful any of them actually expect you to throw yourself at their feet. They're probably concentrating really hard to hear your response because they left their hearing aids at home. Make sure you yell so that they can hear you.

Despite their advancing years, we must remember to honor those who went before us. It would be in bad taste to make fun of these kinky geezers, so try and restrain yourself from giggling at the assortment of whips hanging from their walkers and their insistence on using a Clapper to activate their TENS units. Remember, we'll be old someday, if we're lucky.

SINcerely,

Mistress Dominique

Dear Mistress Dominique,

I'm afraid my marriage of fifteen years is in horrible trouble. Yesterday I cleaned under the bed and found a box my husband had hidden. I couldn't believe what was inside! There were books about something called Korean wire bondage, a book about spanking, a horrid book that looks like it's about drinking people's pee, pamphlets from places that sell hideous torture devices and a lot of catalogs from Sadistic Suzy's House of Rubber. Frankly, I'm frightened that my husband is interested in such terrible activities. He's a hardworking man, a good father and has been active in local Republican Party politics most of his life. Is he sick? What do I do?

Terrified in Memphis

Dear Terrified,

Good lord, of course he's sick! He's twisted to the core and you should get out of that house NOW before he does something dangerous! How could you live with a man that long and not know he is a Republican? Clear out now before he brings Tom Delay home to dinner. Do it, woman! Save yourself!

SINcerely,

Mistress Dominique

Dear Mistress Dominique,

Hey, you kinky chicks are great! I'll bet you got a big rack and a tight ass, baybee. Me and the boys down here at Elroy's Tap wanna know how we can get it on with a hot chick like you. Yeah! Get it on! We dig the leather babes!

Captain Studly

Dear Captain,

How can I refuse such a request? If you want to meet a woman such as myself, follow these simple steps. First, drink lots and lots of beer. Dominant women love a man who can hold his brewskis. Next, go the to nearest large airport and buy a ticket for the first departing flight. Once you are airborne, rush into the cockpit and tell the pilot that unless he lets you out of the plane you will blow it up. When you are escorted to the door, decline any offer of a parachute. Tell them parachutes are for wusses. Then jump out of the plane and wait for the dominant women to beat a path to your door. Good luck!

SINcerely,

Mistress Dominique

Dear Mistress Dominique,

Hey, my friend Ricky, a.k.a. Captain Studly, tried that thing you said about jumping out of a plane and now he's dead. What gives? Me and the rest of the boys are still waiting to get into some leather chick's pants!

Confused

Dear Confused,

Hmmm. Obviously he was not the type of man a dominant woman would want. Follow my instructions yourself and this time get it right.

SINcerely,

Mistress Dominique

Dear Mistress Dominique,

You know what gets me hard? Sometimes my dog goes out in the backyard and eats a squirrel or a badger and then comes back in the house and ralphs it up on the carpet. It doesn't happen too often, but when it does I get so horny I can't stand it and have to whack off. Am I crazy?

Ralphy

Dear Ralphy,

Yes. Yes, you are.

SINcerely,

Mistress Dominique

Dear Mistress Dominique,

I am a lifestyle dominatrix like yourself. My sub is my boyfriend, Ernie, who moved in with me about a month ago. There is nothing I like better than tying Ernie to the whipping post we have out behind the tool shed and giving him a good working over. My problem is the other day, right after I started striping Ernie's back, the doorbell rang. I went to answer the door and it was the UPS man, who had gotten lost trying to deliver a package. As I gave the man directions, I heard Ernie screaming his head off out back but I couldn't figure out why, since I wasn't hitting him at the time.

Imagine my surprise when I discovered that while I was in the house, a wolverine had gotten into the yard and bitten off Ernie's peter. My poor boy was covered in blood and howling something awful. I untied him from the whipping post and took him to the hospital but they kept wanting to know where Ernie's peter was, so I had to drive back and look for it. By then it was getting dark so I didn't have much time to look. Finally, I had to go back to the hospital and tell them it was lost. The surgeon, a man, looked horribly upset but I could swear I saw a couple of nurses giggling.

Well, to make a long story short, a week went by and Ernie was released from the hospital. He's a lot different now, and helps out a lot with the cooking and cleaning, and even redecorated the bedroom. It's been nice, to say the least, like having a girlfriend around all the time.

The problem is, today I was weeding the azaleas and there was Ernie's peter lying in the dirt. It was shriveled up and moldy but I don't know if they could still hook it back up or not. I don't want to tell anyone I found it because things are good as they are, you know? If I keep quiet, does it make me a bad person?

Emotionally torn,

Mistress Rowena

Dear Mistress Rowena,

This is a tough one to answer. Legally, Ernie is entitled to have his man worm back but on the other hand, what he doesn't know won't hurt you, right? If they stick the tallywhacker back on, he'll probably return to sitting on the couch, belching the alphabet and watching stockcar races the way men do. If you like the way things are now, I'd chuck the tadpole in a ditch and keep Ernie in the dark. Hmmm. Artie has been getting uppity lately. Maybe we have wolverines around here as well…

SINcerely,

Mistress Dominique

Dear Mistress Dominique,

Does food turn you on? Man, I can't enough of it! But I don't mean food that you eat. I'm talking about food you smear all over yourself. I love to go to the grocery store and get a bunch of those industrial-sized cans of mayonnaise. Then I go home and get naked, dump the mayo on the floor and jump in there and roll around in it.

Sometimes, if I'm extra horny, I drop a few cans of peas in there too. It's prettier, plus you get a little texture that way and you can really feel it when the peas and mayo get up your ass crack. Yeeah! What do you think of that? Bet you're all wet, huh?

Don't hold the mayo!

Steve

Dear Steve,

No, I'm not all wet. In fact, I'm pissed off. Last week I went to the store for a jar of mayo to mix with my tuna salad but they were out, probably because a freaky bint like you bought it all to roll around in. Jerk. My dogs occasionally roll in their own vomit but they don't get a boner about it. Next time I need a condiment, the shelves better be full or you'll be rolling on a nest of fire ants.

SINcerely,

Mistress Dominique

Dear Mistress Dominique,

My girlfriend and I have been into kinky stuff for a long time. She's the domme and I'm her slave. We've always been intense about our scenes, with lots of bondage and whips. I especially get into verbal humiliation and she's really good at it, but lately she hasn't been as interested in sceneing and says she has "top's disease". What is that? Should I be worried?

Worried slave

Dear Worried,

Of course you should be concerned. I have a friend, Mistress HellWhore, who had top's disease a couple of years ago. It's a terrible thing—wet hacking cough, runny nose, diarrhea, lots of nasty symptoms. One day she was working over some clod in her dungeon and heaved all over the guy. (I guess that's why it's also known as "top drop". Ha ha!) Of course, the clod thought it was vomit play and got a major hard-on, so she kicked him in the jimmies a few times and told him to go home. A week later, she retired as a professional domme and got a job at the DMV, so now she can abuse people without having to look at their hairy nasty bits. If your Mistress hurls on you and starts to talk about an exciting career arguing with people regarding their driver's licenses, I'd say she has top's disease. Good luck.

SINcerely,

Mistress Dominique

Dear Mistress Dominique,

My wife says it would turn her on to no end if I would learn Japanese rope bondage. Well, I've been to every hardware store in town, plus a couple of those home improvement places, and no one carries Japanese rope. What is so special about it, anyway?

Stuck with crummy American rope

Dear Stuck,

You didn't make the honor roll in school, did you? Oh, and if you should decide to write me again, please use a regular sheet of paper. Scrawling a letter in crayon on the back of an International House of Pancakes placemat isn't going to impress many people, especially since it appears like you had trouble keeping the Viva La French Toast in your mouth.

SINcerely,

Mistress Dominique

Dear Mistress Dominique,

You are so hot!!! I saw the pictures on your website and man oh man would I like to meat you. (Get it? Meat you?) Every night before I go to sleep, I masturbate about you. It's always the same fantasy, you know? I'm in the front yard naked and you come charging out of the garage waving a big rake over your head. I can't run fast enough to get away from you because these one-eyed snakes pop out of the ground and grab my ankles. They spit white venom on me and yell shit like, "You can't escape! You're gonna get hit with a rake!" Then it rains clams and everything smells like fish.

Sometimes I get away from the snakes and the clams but then hundreds of army generals dressed like my mother charge out of a cave and try to knock me down. Some of them have guns that shoot cucumbers. (It really hurts when one hits me in the nards, you know?)

Finally, I make it to the street and you're waiting for me but now you're fifty feet tall! And there's a bunch of guys stuck in your black silk panties, screaming for help. You lean down to hit me with the rake, which is now tiny in your giant hand, but a river of urine rushes down the street and washes me away. I look back just in time to see the 1968 Minnesota Twins setting the house on fire while you spit on them. After that, I usually come. Oh yeah!

Hot for you

Dear Hot,

You are one sick puppy. This is one of the most twisted things I've ever heard and that's saying a lot. The 1968 Minnesota Twins? What kind of weird hell is that? Get some help, bud, before you end up in an insane asylum.

SINcerely,

Mistress Dominique

Dear Mistress Dominique,

I've had it up to here with you kinky people. Why can't you have normal relationships without all the weird stuff? My husband started reading all sorts of strangeness on the Internet from people like you and all of a sudden our sex life isn't good enough for him. Noooo, now he says we have to dress up in costumes and act out weird dramas he thinks up.

I got so tired of him nagging me that I finally gave in to his perversion one night just to get some peace. I still can't believe I did this, but I actually put on a Wonder Woman costume he'd gotten and let him tie me to the bed. He left for a while and came back dressed in a Batman outfit. He looked stupid, especially with his potbelly hanging over the utility belt.

The idea was that I'd been captured by a super villain, Brainiac Lord or whoever, and "Batman" would rescue me. Of course, I'd be so grateful that we'd immediately have sex. Duh. I just wanted to get it over with. Anyway, my husband runs in wearing his dumb costume and shouting about defeating the Brain guy when he suddenly stopped and stared out the window. His eyeballs got big then he yelled something about a bat signal and ran from the room. A minute later, I heard the car start and go screeching down the street. After that, nothing, and I do mean nothing. I laid there for two days waiting for that bonehead to come back and untie me. Finally, I started yelling and the neighbors broke in and let me go. It was so embarrassing and what a mess!

I hope you and your kinky friends are happy. My life is now a living hell. That stupid fool I married never came back and every time I talk to the police, they laugh and hang up on me. I wish I knew who to sue because I'd do it in a heartbeat. You're all a bunch of sick perverts!

Really Disgusted

Dear Really Disgusted,

I must admit, you do have a point. Wearing a Batman costume is so last year! No wonder the experience was bad for you. On the other hand, you can take heart in the fact that Bat Boy is probably in jail somewhere on a lewd conduct charge. Maybe some of his fellow prisoners have their own scenes they want to act out. Heh heh.

SINcerely,

Mistress Dominique

Dear Mistress Dominique,

A couple of years ago my husband confessed to cross-dressing when I wasn't around. It was hard to take at first but eventually I got used to the idea and we even started having some fun with it. Okay, I got turned on buying him a girdle or a slip at Penney's because I knew how hot he would be when I made him wear them.

Unfortunately, we have a new problem. It's not enough that he cross-dresses. Now he wants to look like that Morticia woman from The Addams Family. That's just too much! It's creepy and besides, he doesn't have the figure for it. Plus, I'm afraid he'll start eating spiders or something. Help!

Perplexed Wife

Dear Perplexed,

You know, I once had a male slave who thought he could please me by dressing up as my fellow advice columnist, Dear Abby. When he was all rigged out he looked a lot like my mother, which creeped me out. It wasn't that I couldn't bring myself to whip him or put him in extreme bondage. The problem was that I liked it way too much. I loved torturing the old hag! I got so carried away with my Burmese steel-tipped flogger that I almost ripped the skin off her back. I mean, his *back.*

I guess that has nothing to do with your problem but that's the way it goes sometimes. Good luck.

SINcerely,

Mistress Dominique

Dear Mistress Dominique,

A good friend of mine, a dominatrix, is getting married to her favorite male slave. She has honored me by asking that I serve as the Domme of Honor. My problem is that I don't know what my responsibilities are during the ceremony. Can you help?

Mistress Icebox, Cold Queen of the Northeast

Dear Mistress Icebox,

You are indeed honored by your fellow Domme's request. First of all, understand that since this is a solemn ceremony, formal black leather is required – no latex, spandex or metalwear, and certainly no nudity, unless specifically requested by the bride.

Even we Dommes get jittery about our wedding day, so make it your responsibility to ensure that everything goes smoothly. In addition to the usual Domme of Honor chores, you may be asked to hold the slave's leash or perhaps kick him in the nards as he approaches the altar, so that he knows he is to assume a kneeling position. You may be asked to pierce the slave's genitals or cane the slave during certain parts of the ceremony, particularly when a howl of pain is required. At the completion of the service, you will most certainly be involved in the ritual beating and kicking of the slave groom as he attempts to crawl from the altar and down the aisle. You will also be responsible for making the wedding toast at the reception and smashing the first bottle of champagne over the slave's head.

It sounds like fun, right? Of course it is, so enjoy yourself and help make the day special for your friend as she enters into the scared bonds of matrimony, or handfasting, or voodoo, or whatever the hell they're doing.

SINcerely,

Mistress Dominique

Chapter Ten
Kinky Aptitude Test

FIND YOUR KINK KWOTIENT!!

Okay, you've read this far and learned quite a bit about kinky people, their behavior, their culture and the implements they use to inflict both pain and pleasure on one another. Chances are, most of you are horrified at what you've read but some of you may be asking yourself, "Hey, this stuff looks like fun! Am I kinky too?" Well, why not find out? The following is a questionnaire designed to ascertain your relative level of kinkiness. I'd like to thank Miss Lola Vaught, who teaches a home economics course for prisoners at a nearby penitentiary, for her invaluable help in constructing this quiz.

1. What flavor of ice cream best describes your sexual persona?

A. Vanilla

B. Chocolate

C. Rocky Road

D. Fudge Nut Ripple

2. Complete this sentence: My spouse doesn't understand me because I like to __________.

A. tie people up

B. run around in rubber clothing

C. collect and maintain old Spiro Agnew watches

D. put on a frilly dress and be called Shirley

3. Which of the following is an appropriate implement for a whipping scene?

A. Toaster

B. Small dog

C. Taiwanese spiked flogger

D. Pick axe

4. Which movie would you most like to watch?

A. The History of Wallpaper

B. Captain Billy's Barge from Hell

C. Mistress Susan, Queen of Steel Bondage

D. The Radish That Ate Pittsburgh

5. Which is the most sensual to touch?

A. Leather

B. Broken glass

C. Old pudding

D. Tree bark

6. It's Friday night. The kids are staying over at their Grandmother's house, the dog has been fed and we have the whole evening to do what we want. The first thing that enters my mind is __________ .

A. doing the dishes

B. balancing the checkbook

C. reading a book about the history of wallpaper

D. pouring industrial-sized cans of minestrone all over the living room floor and having wild sex while dressed as naughty accountants

7. Which of the following items has the most potential for kinky usage?

A. Can opener

B. Old copy of *TV Guide* with a completed crossword puzzle

C. Box of tissues

D. One of those AOL CDs that show up in the mail every other day

8. A good name for a dominatrix would be

A. Mistress Canker

B. Lady Fatal, Mistress of Instant Death

C. Babs, Empress of Lint

D. Skippy

9. You are a dominant who likes to roleplay as a strong and strict schoolteacher. The role you would most like your submissive to assume is:

A. An equally strong and strict school teacher.

B. The person who delivers the dead frogs for biology class.

C. An honor student who stays after school to clean the erasers.

D. A math teacher who has gone astray.

10. You arrive home from work and discover your spouse lounging on the sofa, dressed as Cleopatra and clasping a largish whip. Your reaction is:

A. Abject terror, as you have a phobia about Cleopatra impersonators.

B. Anger, because you know he's ruined your best eyeliner pencil again.

C. Confusion, since you don't have a spouse.

D. Woohoo!

11. What is the kinkiest item you can buy at Kmart?

A. Blender

B. Battery cables

C. Some of those Martha Stewart sheets

D. Adult diapers

12. Which of the following would be your most likely kinky fantasy?

A. Having sex in a public place.

B. Having sex with a game show host.

C. Having sex with a game show host in a public place.

D. That Cleopatra thing sounded pretty good.

13. You decide to wear something naughty. What would that be?

A. Bib overalls and a plaid shirt.

B. Your birthday suit.

C. Something you snuck from my mother's closet.

D. Spurs. Just spurs.

14. Which is the best example of scene music?

A. Mantovani

B. Tesh! Tesh! Tesh!

C. The Archies

D. The Royal English Dragoons Marching Bagpipes Band

15. What is subspace?

A. The cabinet under the sink where you keep your subs.

B. Something to do with submarines, I guess.

C. A feeling submissives get when they are tied up, gagged and thrown into the trunk of a car.

D. One of those Star Trek or Star Wars things, like when they take a shortcut through space because some guy with three heads and four buttocks is chasing them so he can sell them new siding for their spaceship. Something like that.

16. Which of the scenes below is the biggest turn-on for you?

A. Prisoner of war tortured by vicious Canadians.

B. Clerk at a convenience store taken hostage by militant Girl Scouts.

C. Helpless victim of a group of women dressed as wolverines.

D. Door-to-door vacuum cleaner salesperson who falls down a lot.

17. Who of the following would you say is the best role model for a dominant?

A. Bill Cosby

B. PeeWee Herman

C. Jack Nicklaus

D. Former United States Secretary of Agriculture Dan Glickman

18. Every well-equipped dungeon should include:

A. Newer magazines than in the dentist's office.

B. A black light poster of those dogs playing poker.

C. Appropriate aperitifs and a nice chilled Chardonnay.

D. Tweezers.

19. Which of the following is the best way to meet a suitable play partner?

A. Go to a local sex club dressed as a Pokémon character.

B. Call random numbers in the phone book and whisper "I like rubber" over and over until you get a positive reaction.

C. Ask your local clergy if he or she knows anyone "hip to the scene".

D. Buy a leather posture collar and wear it around town until someone

mentions it.

20. The slogan used to describe ethical behavior in the BDSM community is: "Safe, sane and __________."

A. moist

B. silly

C. dangerous

D.partly cloudy with a chance of evening thundershowers

SCORING:

To compute your score, you must be knowledgeable in bivariate statistical analysis. A familiarity with nonlinear regression analysis and computer software capable of calculating an appropriate curve fitting program are also necessary. If you don't have the requisite skills or computer equipment, you really shouldn't have taken the test in the first place.

Epilogue

The research is finished and you now know everything you need to know about kink. I can't help but wonder if anyone will decide to be kinky after reading this. That's a scary thought—my being responsible for altering the lifestyles of my readers. I must warn you that being kinky is fraught with peril, so do so at your own risk. Come to think of it, being an ethnographer is a risky business as well. If I've learned nothing else, I know that immersing oneself in the lives of others carries serious consequences.

I have not become kinky as a result of my ethnological adventures. I wish I could say that life goes on now just as it did before I began this enterprise, but sadly, that is not the case. I am no longer welcome at the meetings of the Rocking Robins, the Harold Leipnitz Film Appreciation Society, the Savvy Seeders or any group to which I previously belonged. I sent them all letters explaining my project but it did no good. They remain convinced that I'm a monstrous pervert roaming the streets at night, dressed in rubber and waving a cat-o'-nine-tails at innocent strangers.

I've changed my phone number several times since I ran the newspaper advertisement from Mistress Dominique but that Dick person always finds me. He calls late at night, breathing heavily and then shouting incoherently when I say his name. I got so fed up with the man that I answered the phone one night by yelling, "Dick! Dick! Dick! Is that enough Dick for you?" The caller turned out to be Pastor George, the replacement for Pastor Herman at the First United Presbyterian church. What a mess that turned out to be. I'm told my services are no longer wanted at the annual Women's Auxiliary Bake Sale. They also strongly suggested I begin attending services at the Lutheran church, where, they said, perverted activities are much more welcome.

Thankfully, I'm still close to Aunt Ruth, though she's rarely at home these days. It seems like I'm always house-sitting her plants and collecting her mail while she's off adventuring with Juan or Carlos or Juan Carlos or Pepe, whoever she's seeing at the moment.

My mother tried to force me to get counseling, even after I explained what I was doing. "No daughter of mine is going to ruin our family name running about with deviants and fiends!" she howls, and there's no calming her down once she gets started. I'm still invited to dinner on Sunday nights but one of the other guests invariably turns out to be a local psychiatrist or psychologist who ruins the meal by asking me innumerable questions about my childhood and potty training.

Sadly, I never discovered what happened to dear Uncle Henry. I miss him so. An incident occurred recently that made me think of him and his collection of kinky materials still sitting in my basement. A package arrived at my home in a plain brown wrapper with no return address. Inside I found a DVD and an unsigned note:

Hey, Annabelle! I hear great things about you these days. Glad to see there's at least one person in the family who isn't a boring, self-righteous poop. I hope you enjoy this show as much as I enjoyed making it. Perv power!

The enclosed DVD was titled *Whip Fest 5000!* The plot, what there was of it, concerned the activities of people from a kinky planet three thousand years from now. The futuristic sets weren't convincing, though the fetish costuming was quite good. Most of the action involved spankings and whippings, leading up to the dramatic climax when the kinky people discovered a badly made papier-mâché model of the Statue of Liberty—wielding a whip instead of a torch—sticking halfway out of a desolate beach. At that point, they realized they were still on Earth and began a fresh round of whipping right there on the sand.

The last scene depicted a man in leather chaps leaning over to expose his bare buttocks to the queen of the kinky people. As she began lashing the tar out of him, the camera zoomed to a close-up of the man's face, hidden behind a leather bondage mask. He looked right into the camera as the punishment continued and he winked.

That wink looked familiar, somehow, and I got the strangest feeling the wink was meant for me.

What a silly idea.

Enjoy an excerpt from:

Walking On the Moon

ꟸ

"You mean it's alcoholic?" Morrison asked in shock, and slid under the checkered tablecloth. "Ouzo is liquor?"

They'd been passing the ouzo bottles to slake their thirst for nearly an hour. Hand-loading a cargo hauler was mighty thirsty work.

"Tastes like licorice-flavored tar," Cleary contributed, voice slurred. He held up his half-full bottle. "I like it."

"I've never had real alcohol before," Fox said. "You know, this planet looks funny." He squinted, peering into the distance. The flat-roofed houses, the big pots of red flowers bordering the perimeter of the outdoor cafe where they sat, the boats in the harbor below all wavered hazily in and out of focus.

"Are we drunk?" Toffler questioned.

"Not like a happy pill," Harcort contributed.

Sakretis smiled benignly. "No, it isn't. These ancestors of mine have a good thing here." He poked a fragrant mound on his plate. "This grape leaf stuff is good too. But it's not chili," he added wistfully. "I could really go for a bowl of chili."

"Me too," several voices chimed in.

It took him a couple of tries, but Morrison managed to pull himself out from under the table. "Where's Duchamp? My legs are all funny."

"Took a walk by the water," Fox said. "New Sydney's a water world. He's homesick. I like the desert. Heat." He licked his lips. "Chili."

"I've got an idea," Cleary declared, climbing unsteadily to his feet. "Let's go grocery shopping while everybody's still asleep. Sleepray's a wonderful thing," he added. "While everyone's asleep we can raid the commissary we saw up the street. Take back some real food."

"Duchamp won't like that," Harcort said.

"Don't have to tell him," Fox contributed.

"We got an empty storage chest on the shuttle," Morrison added encouragingly.

"Let's do it," Sakretis assented.

"Yeah," Toffler chimed in, then gulped down the rest of the bottle of ouzo.

They wobbled to their feet and trooped drunkenly a few doors up the street. All was quiet and dark inside the little store. They found baskets and began filling them with anything on the shelves that looked like it might be food. Not that the crew's vision or judgment was any too clear by this time.

They laughed and joked and made two trips to the shuttle, and were back for a third when the door opened behind them. Cans and bags crashed noisily to the floor as three of the drunken crewmen went for their sleeprays while the others began to speak all at once.

"Duchamp!"

"We'll put it back!"

"We'll leave cash for the supplies!"

"That's not Duchamp!" Fox declared.

Long seconds went by as they came to realize there was a startled woman standing in the shaft of sunlight by the open door.

She was a vision.

The answer to a hungry, drunken man's dreams.

Six desperate men suddenly believed there was indeed justice in the universe.

"It's her!"

"Claudia!"

"Chili!"

"Get her!" Cleary shouted.

Three sleeprays fired as one.

* * * * *

"Where have you been?" Denys demanded as he climbed into the shuttle from the storage bay's rear entrance.

He'd looked all over the small village for his shift crew before giving up and heading back to use the ship's recall signal. The last place he'd expected to find the crewmen was where they were supposed to be.

Three of them sat down hastily on a storage chest as he entered.

The other three started guiltily as he came toward them. Cleary gave him an innocent grin. The one he always gave when he was up to something.

Fox began tunelessly whistling. They all smelled of alcohol. *Hmmm.* Denys rubbed his chin as he tried to decide whether or not to find out what they'd just stowed in the chest. *It's food,* he decided. It's what he would have pilfered if his shift officer had left him on his own long enough.

Should he confiscate it? Did they have time? There was a wide-awake woman running around Doros. She'd probably noticed a few sleeping citizens by now. Why hadn't he thought to put her under? It wouldn't have hurt her. He felt a pang of guilt for something he hadn't even done to Claudia Cameron. It would have just put her to sleep—but it would have seemed too much like hurting her, or cheating her. *Never mind Claudia Cameron. Think of duty. It's better to just get out of here,* he decided. Away from Claudia. He'd already had too many thoughts about the woman from the cooking show, even before he met her. Having met her, all he could do was flee the scene before he had an urge to grab her and bring her back to the ship to warm his nights with something more than her spicy cooking.

To keep from thinking about that improper fantasy, he looked sternly at his men. "You better have paid for whatever you took," he told the crew.

Several of them turned various shades of red. There were several nods. Fox's eyes closed and he quietly passed out. The men had either not done the required research about twenty-first century Earth, or they had and had decided to try out some of the available stimulants. Duchamp sighed. Good thing he was the designated driver.

"Let's get these supplies to the HATTON. Strap in."

"Yes, sir!" five voices declared enthusiastically. Fox began gently snoring as Harcort and Sakretis carried him into the passenger compartment. Denys followed after them, thinking how glad he'd be to get this mission over and get back home to the twenty-third century.

Why an electronic book?

We live in the Information Age—an exciting time in the history of human civilization, in which technology rules supreme and continues to progress in leaps and bounds every minute of every day. For a multitude of reasons, more and more avid literary fans are opting to purchase e-books instead of paper books. The question from those not yet initiated into the world of electronic reading is simply: *Why?*

1. ***Price.*** An electronic title at Ellora's Cave Publishing and Cerridwen Press runs anywhere from 40% to 75% less than the cover price of the exact same title in paperback format. Why? Basic mathematics and cost. It is less expensive to publish an e-book (no paper and printing, no warehousing and shipping) than it is to publish a paperback, so the savings are passed along to the consumer.
2. ***Space.*** Running out of room in your house for your books? That is one worry you will never have with electronic books. For a low one-time cost, you can purchase a handheld device specifically designed for e-reading. Many e-readers have large, convenient screens for viewing. Better yet, hundreds of titles can be stored within your new library—on a single microchip. There are a variety of e-readers from different manufacturers. You can also read e-books on your PC or laptop computer. (Please note that Ellora's

Cave does not endorse any specific brands. You can check our websites at www.ellorascave.com or www.cerridwenpress.com for information we make available to new consumers.)

3. ***Mobility***. Because your new e-library consists of only a microchip within a small, easily transportable e-reader, your entire cache of books can be taken with you wherever you go.
4. ***Personal Viewing Preferences.*** Are the words you are currently reading too small? Too large? Too... ANNOYING? Paperback books cannot be modified according to personal preferences, but e-books can.
5. ***Instant Gratification.*** Is it the middle of the night and all the bookstores near you are closed? Are you tired of waiting days, sometimes weeks, for bookstores to ship the novels you bought? Ellora's Cave Publishing sells instantaneous downloads twenty-four hours a day, seven days a week, every day of the year. Our webstore is never closed. Our e-book delivery system is 100% automated, meaning your order is filled as soon as you pay for it.

Those are a few of the top reasons why electronic books are replacing paperbacks for many avid readers.

As always, Ellora's Cave and Cerridwen Press welcome your questions and comments. We invite you to email us at Comments@ellorascave.com or write to us directly at Ellora's Cave Publishing Inc., 1056 Home Avenue, Akron, OH 44310-3502.

Cerridwen Press

Hocus Pocus

By Teresa Roblin

Shy and quiet Amanda Santorelli is unhappy watching the world go by around her. When her well-meaning but wacky aunt casts an assertiveness spell on her, Amanda's orderly world is turned upside down. Unable to control herself, Amanda blurts out whatever is on her mind every time someone asks her a question. Trying to outwit the spell only makes matters worse. With no control over her own mouth, it's only a matter of time before someone discovers the object of her secret obsession.

Mark Abbott is happy with the way his unassuming assistant runs his office. But all of a sudden she's become a new person—both in attitude and appearance—and he's not sure he likes the effect on his orderly work routine. With each passing day, he finds himself waiting to see what will come out of her mouth next. Before long, he can no longer deny the truth—the new Amanda is seriously making him reconsider his vow never to mix business with pleasure.

Mark doesn't know if it's love—or if he's just a victim of Hocus Pocus.

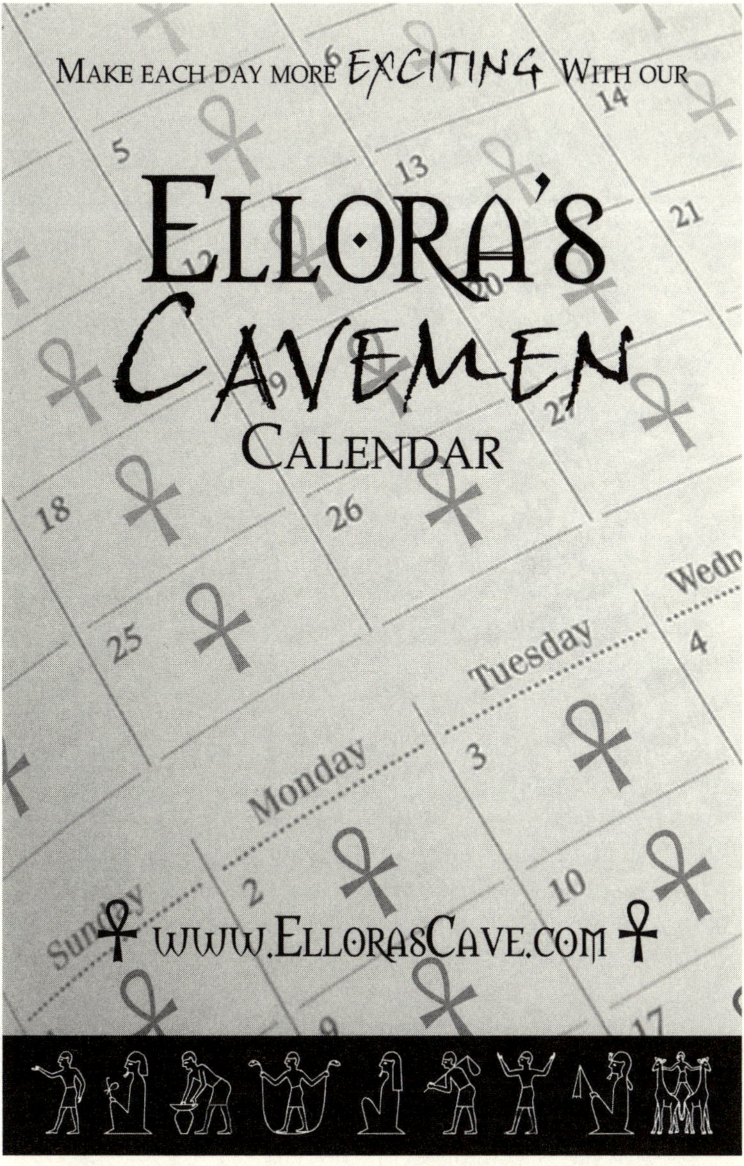
Make each day more EXCITING With our
Ellora's
Cavemen
Calendar
www.EllorasCave.com